PRAISE FOR

Wanda Seasongood and the Mostly True Secret

"In her amazing journey through the Scary Wood, Wanda Seasongood fades to smoke, nearly drowns, is torn limb from limb, turns into a squid, and almost explodes. And that's just the BEGINNING! Come along with her on **a sly, laugh-out-loud adventure** you'll never forget."
—R. L. Stine, bestselling author of the Goosebumps series

"[Susan] Lurie spins a tale with **satisfying twists and turns** to keep the reader wondering who, if anyone, can be trusted in this fantastical adventure." —*The Bulletin*

"Readers will find it hard to put this book down once they start reading and will be excited to find out what's next for Wanda and Voltaire." —*School Library Journal*

"Wanda is by turns charmingly flabbergasted and persistently practical but ever well meaning; **readers are sure to root for her along the journey.**"
—*Kirkus Reviews*

"Readers will revel in the **fantastical creatures and supernatural elements** while cheering for Wanda and her avian sidekick." —*Booklist*

Wanda Seasongood
and the
Mostly True Secret

BY Susan Lurie

ILLUSTRATED BY Jenn Harney

LITTLE, BROWN AND COMPANY

New York Boston

Text copyright © 2020 by Susan Lurie
Illustrations copyright © 2020 by Jennifer Harney
Text in excerpt from *Wanda Seasongood and the Almost Perfect Lie* copyright © 2020 by Susan Lurie
Illustrations in excerpt from *Wanda Seasongood and the Almost Perfect Lie* copyright © 2020 by Jennifer Harney

Cover art copyright © 2020 by Jennifer Harney. Cover design by Tyler Nevins and Jennifer Harney. Cover copyright © 2020 by Hachette Book Group, Inc.

Little, Brown and Company
Hachette Book Group
1290 Avenue of the Americas, New York, NY 10104
Visit us at LBYR.com

Originally published in hardcover and ebook by Disney • Hyperion, an imprint of Disney Book Group, in February 2020
First Trade Paperback Edition: February 2021

Little, Brown and Company is a division of Hachette Book Group, Inc. The Little, Brown name and logo are trademarks of Hachette Book Group, Inc.

The publisher is not responsible for websites (or their content) that are not owned by the publisher.

The Library of Congress has cataloged the hardcover edition as follows:
Names: Lurie, Susan (Susan L.), author. • Harney, Jennifer, illustrator.
Title: Wanda Seasongood and the mostly true secret / by Susan Lurie ; illustrated by Jenn Harney.
Description: First edition. • Los Angeles ; New York : Disney - Hyperion, 2020. • Summary: "Wanda doesn't fit in with her family and is always searching for clues about her past. On her eleventh birthday, a talking bluebird named Voltaire shows up and takes her on a quest through the Scary Wood to find her true parents"— Provided by publisher.
Identifiers: LCCN 2018026164 • ISBN 9781368043151
Subjects: • CYAC: Identity—Fiction. • Witches—Fiction. • Magic—Fiction. • Brothers and sisters—Fiction. • Bluebirds—Fiction. • Memory—Fiction.
Classification: LCC PZ7.1.L87 Wan 2020 • DDC [Fic]—dc23
LC record available at https://lccn.loc.gov/2018026164

ISBNs: 978-0-7595-5616-4 (pbk.), 978-1-368-05429-4 (ebook),

Printed in the United States of America

LSC-C

Printing 1, 2020

*For my mother, who lives on
every page of this book.*

For my father, an extraordinary adventurer.

And always, in all ways, for Lou.

ONE

It Started with a Thud

On Wanda Seasongood's eleventh birthday, a bright and bouncy bluebird flew toward her bedroom window. *Just like in a fairy tale,* she thought as she watched it flutter her way. But the window wasn't open, and the little bird's head smacked into the glass, making quite a thud. Then it dropped, lifeless, into the tangled garden below.

That was Wanda's first birthday surprise.

Wanda hoped against reason that the bird was all right. She ran from her room and leaped down the stairs, two at a time, her frizzy reddish-brown hair flying behind her.

"Wanda, where are you going?" her mother shouted

from the kitchen. "Such a racket you're making! You'll drive Zane crazy."

Zane was Wanda's horrible eight-year-old brother, and quite frankly, he was already crazy. He kicked things and howled all day long, and her parents could not restrain him. And yet they only had praise for him. They yelled at Wanda for all the awful things he did. And they demanded that she take him wherever she went. Which is why Wanda had no friends, not even one.

When Wanda reached the bottom of the stairs, her parents were waiting for her, with Zane standing squarely in front of them. His wavy dark hair was matted with dirt. He glared at Wanda with his cold blue eyes.

"I'm just going into the yard," Wanda said.

"Take him with you." Her mother's hands rested on Zane's shoulders. "He needs some fresh air."

"Yes," her father added. "Besides, it's your turn to watch him."

Wanda's shoulders sagged. It *always* seemed to be her turn. "Come on, Zane." She gently took his hand—

And he bit her arm.

"Ow!" she cried, pulling away and spotting his teeth marks clearly pressed into her skin.

"Wanda, why did you grab him so tightly?" her mother scolded.

"When will you learn?" Her father shook his head in disgust.

"*When will you learn, Wanda?*" Zane shrieked with glee. "*When will you learn?*" He stomped on her foot and bolted out the front door.

Zane ran into the street. Into the path of an oncoming car. It braked with a loud screech, but Zane just giggled. He continued to the other side and promptly started yanking leaves off the neighbors' shrubs.

"Now look what you've done, Wanda!" Her mother's cheeks flushed with anger.

Wanda swallowed the hurt, as she was accustomed to doing, and watched her parents take off after Zane. Then she rushed through the kitchen and into the yard to search for the bluebird.

I hope I'm not too late. She tore through the creeping thistle that choked the garden. Its spiky leaves cut her hands as she parted the stalks, searching for the little bird.

Please don't be dead. Please don't be dead. Not on my birthday. That would be such bad luck, Wanda thought. As she combed through the plants, her eyeglasses, large brown frames perched on her freckled nose, slipped down until she was peering over them.

"There you are!" She finally caught a glimpse of the

bird's feathers. She could tell it was a male from his bright blue color. A note was tied around his neck, but Wanda didn't see it at first.

She pushed her glasses up, stared at the bird for a moment, and let out a long, heavy sigh.

"Happy birthday, Wanda," she said. "Here's a dead bird to help you celebrate." She poked the bird with her pinkie. "Well, I guess it won't be having any cake."

The truth was, Wanda wouldn't be having any cake, either. Her parents always forgot her birthday. But she still planned on lighting a candle so she could make the wish she'd been wishing on every birthday for as long as she could remember.

Wanda lived at the foot of the Catskill Mountains. When she was six, she had heard the tale of a man named Rip Van Winkle, and that's when this wish had taken shape and burrowed into the chambers of her heart.

Rip lived in the Catskill Mountains, too, and one day he took a nap in the woods. When he awakened, everything had changed. It seemed he had slept for twenty years.

The moment Wanda heard this story, she wished that she, too, would fall into an enchanted sleep, and when she awakened, she would also find that everything had changed. She would discover, much to her delight, that she was an orphan, free of Zane and her parents.

Now, if you've ever made wishes, birthday or otherwise, you know they're usually as light as a petal and as smooth as silk. They sparkle and shimmer, and the mere thought of them can send you whirling like a dervish.

Most of Wanda's wishes were like that. But not this one. This one was heavy and dark, and her shoulders slumped under the weight of it. But on each birthday, she made the wish with greater conviction and increased fervor. And to be absolutely clear about it, she would add, "Disappearance is preferred, but dead would be okay, too."

On first hearing, and probably second and third, that might seem like a cold, harsh wish, and it might turn you against Wanda—but it shouldn't. Wanda's brother truly was a beast of a boy. He ate with his hands, chomped loudly on his food, and let it dribble down his chin.

When asked politely to pass the peas, he'd help himself first, fill his mouth to brimming, then spit them onto her plate. He blew his nose in Wanda's best dresses. He never combed his bushy brown hair. Never brushed his teeth. Never took a bath. When he was especially muddy, he slept in Wanda's bed instead of his own. Shoes and all. And he bit her whenever he had the chance.

And where were Wanda's parents through all this?

Did they ever reprimand Zane, as any reasonable parent would? Did they even once offer their good daughter kind and soothing words?

No. They blamed her instead. They blamed her for all of Zane's bad behavior. Tossing the breakfast bowls out with the trash. Watering the plants with vinegar. Once even setting the kitchen curtains on fire. How could they believe for an instant that Wanda was behind these things? It was bewildering.

Zane was allowed to do whatever he pleased, and their parents were pleased with whatever he did.

Wanda could not make any sense of it. She seemed to

remember a time when her life was brighter. But when she tried to recall those moments, her memory clouded and she could not pierce the fog. No, this dark life was hers and always had been. So she wished and wished and wished.

And while she waited for her wish to come true, did she mope and moan about how unfair her life was? No, not Wanda. Which was very admirable, you'd have to agree. Wanda had the good sense to go her own way. Each afternoon, when she returned from school, she'd lock herself in her bedroom, tend to her homework, then paint or write in her diary. And she found another excellent way to escape. She'd read and read and read, sometimes two or three books at a time. Schoolbooks, novels from the library, the classics on her parents' bookshelves, she'd read them all.

Or, sometimes, if no one was home, she'd snoop.

She'd look in every drawer. In every closet and cupboard. Under every loose floorboard and behind every sooty fireplace brick. Wanda was so different from the three people she lived with, she was certain that a secret kept her imprisoned with them, and if she could find a single clue, even a tiny one, she could venture forth and search for her real family.

But today was Saturday and everyone was home, so there would be no snooping.

And it was Wanda's birthday.

And a dead bluebird sat at her feet.

She looked at him and sighed another long sigh—and the bluebird's head suddenly popped up.

He hopped to his feet, wobbling a bit on his spindly bird legs. He stared at her for a moment, then shook his head, as if to clear it.

"I thought you were dead!" Wanda cried out.

"I thought I was, too," the bird replied.

That was Wanda's second birthday surprise.

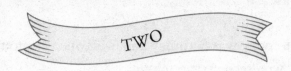

TWO

Have You Been Waiting for a Secret?

"Eeiii!" Wanda shrieked. "You can speak!"

"Evidently," the bird said calmly. He slowly turned, taking one small step after another, making a complete circle, observing his surroundings.

"Nice garden. Somewhat overgrown," he said, opening and closing his small black eyes, trying to focus. "I'm sorry, but I'm feeling a bit dizzy." He gazed down to find a soft place to sit—and caught sight of his matted feathers, crusty and coated with blood.

"What happened to me?" His voice rose in alarm. He searched Wanda's face for an answer and his glance fell to her cut, bloodied hands. He leaped back in a flurry of feathers. "Did you try to kill me?"

"No! No!" Wanda said. "I cut my hands on the thistle. You flew into my window." Wanda pointed to her bedroom above. "Don't you remember?"

"No, I don't." He glanced up at the window, then eyed her suspiciously. "What proof do you have?"

"I would never want to hurt anything," Wanda said, peeved that the bird could think ill of her. "Except for my brother and parents, who I wish were dead," she admitted, feeling absolutely dreadful just saying those words. But if nothing else, Wanda was honest.

"All right, then," the little bird said. "I choose to believe you." But he took a small hop away. "Let's get on with it."

"Let's get on with what?" Wanda's eyes narrowed in confusion.

"The mission, of course," he said. "I'm on an important mission. And there's no time to waste." In a flash, his body stiffened and the bird suddenly appeared alert. Then, just as quickly, he let out a *whoosh* of air so great, he seemed to shrink. "If only I could remember what the mission was . . ."

Wanda watched the bird as he paced back and forth, trying to recall what it was he was supposed to be doing. And that's when Wanda saw it—the note, tucked under a thin vine that was tied around his neck.

"Would it have something to do with that paper you're carrying?" She pointed to the note.

"Yes! That's it!" The bird leaped up with joy. "You are a clever one. I'm supposed to deliver this secret tied around my neck!" His blue-feathered chest puffed out with confidence and pride. "I'm supposed to deliver this secret to—" Then his body slumped. "I'm not really sure. . . ."

"Don't feel bad." Wanda tried to cheer up the bird. "I bet it's hard to remember things with a brain as small as yours." As soon as these words were said, she knew she'd made a big mistake.

But the bird didn't seem to hear her. He concentrated hard, trying to remember. "Who am I supposed to deliver this to? Who? Who?" He pecked the ground with his beak in an effort to jog his memory. "I'm sure I was sure I knew who it was when I started out, but now I'm not sure at all.

"Wait! I know!" His face lit up. "It must be you, because, well, here I am. Have you been waiting for a secret?"

THREE

Read It! Read It!

"Yes! Yes! I *have* been waiting for a secret!" Wanda was astounded by the bird's words.

"Well then," the bird said, lifting a foot to scratch his head. "That means that you must be the One, and if you are the One, then you should read this message tied around my neck."

The secret that had escaped her for so long was now just a fingertip away. Wanda jumped up and flung her arms wide, as if she were about to take flight. Today was her birthday, and even though there would be no cake or song, she knew she would remember this as her best birthday by far. She reached out to the bird to take the note.

"Whoa! Steady there." The bird quickly hopped a few steps back. "What if I'm wrong? What if you aren't the One?"

"But I'm sure I am," Wanda said. The muscles in her forehead twitched, and her brow creased with concern. "I'm absolutely certain of it."

"Hmm . . . Doubt is not a pleasant condition. But certainty is an absurd one," the little bird said.

"Who said *that*?" Wanda asked, because she didn't think the small bird was capable of such a grand thought.

"I did," the bird replied. "My name is Voltaire, and that is my saying."

"Voltaire?" Wanda laughed. "You aren't Voltaire. Voltaire was a French writer from the 1700s. I've read all about him. He was a wise, witty person who wrote plays and poems and novels. A writer of great fame."

"Well, I am a bird of great distinction." The bird ruffled his feathers. "My name is Voltaire."

Wanda didn't know what to make of this creature—a bird who could talk and quote the famous writer Voltaire. If she had tried to get to the bottom of this, it might have saved her from certain danger to come. But rather than prolong the discussion or argue with the bird, Wanda thought it best to turn their attention to what mattered most—the note.

"I know how we can settle this," she told the bird. "The secret I am waiting for will tell me where I truly belong. Is that what the note says?" Wanda's heart skipped with anticipation.

The bird peered up, then side to side. Wanda held her breath and tried not to fidget while she waited for his reply.

Finally, he spoke. "I don't know," he said. "I can't seem to remember. I know I knew it when I left, but now I know I don't know it all." He exhaled a wobbly whistle of a wheeze. "How about we just read the note?"

Wanda reached for it quickly and pulled it away before the bird could change his mind.

Her fingers trembled as she unfolded the tiny piece of paper. She stared at the words, and her mouth turned down in dismay.

"Well, what does it say?" The bird flapped his wings. "Read it! Read it!"

Wanda gazed up from the note. She shook her head. "It says, 'The bird will tell you a secret.'"

FOUR

But How?

Voltaire leaped up from the ground. His small wings beat furiously as he rose in the air. "All right, then!" he cheered. "We're making progress at last!" His head jerked this way and that. He appeared to be searching for something that kept bolting from view.

Could there be more to this message than I realize? Wanda brightened at the thought. She followed the bird's frantic glances. "What are you looking for?" she asked.

"For the bird! For the bird!" Voltaire squawked. "I'm looking for the bird who knows the secret!"

"Oh."

Anyone, even a bird as befuddled as Voltaire, would

have been able to hear Wanda's deep disappointment. His wings stopped beating, and he crashed to the ground. "I see. I see now. I am that bird."

Wanda flopped down on a rock beside the bird and rested her head in her hands. "Well, I suppose this is simply not meant to be. If there *is* a secret, it's not mine to discover."

"Utter nonsense." Voltaire hopped up on her knee. "I don't know you very well. Come to think of it, I don't know you at all. But you don't seem the surrendering sort. And of course there's a secret. And of course it's for you. We just need to find it."

Wanda liked the sound of that. She lifted her head and smiled. "Yes! Let's find it." Then matters of practicality set in, and her head drooped once more. "But how?"

"But how? But how?" The bird's little feet paced up and down Wanda's leg. "I've got it!" He halted his mini march. "We will head into the woods. We will follow the path I traveled, and the secret will return to me. It makes perfect sense. When I left, I knew the secret. When I arrived here, I didn't. That means I lost it somewhere in between. And that spot in between is the woods. So that is where we will go."

Wanda shook her head. "No. I don't think so. I don't think that will work." She let out a sigh, and if a sigh could hold all the sadness in the world, this one did. "I know you are trying to help, but it's useless. I think I am doomed to live this terrible life forever."

"Well," the bird said with a huff, "I think you are feeling sorry for yourself. And what's worse—I think you *like* feeling sorry for yourself!"

"That isn't true!" Wanda leaped from the rock, catapulting the bird into the air.

And it wasn't. Wanda wasn't given to long periods of moping. She had simply briefly lost hope. These things happen.

"That isn't true at all." She said it again to be perfectly clear.

"If you say so." Voltaire shrugged. "But the longer we dwell on our misfortunes, the greater is their power to harm us. So let us *do* something about them and set off on our little journey."

Wanda thought about Voltaire's words, and she knew he was right. Because, lately, the more she thought about her terrible life, the more helpless she felt. And *that* feeling felt worst of all.

But still Wanda hesitated. Was the bird's secret really meant for her? Had he ever known it? Could he really remember it with a simple walk in the woods?

Wanda answered those questions with a *no, no,* and

no. The three little *noes* echoed and bounced and banged about in her head.

But the bird wouldn't give up. He might have forgotten the secret, but it seemed to Wanda that he was somehow certain that the woods held the clues he was seeking. And it was almost as if something was compelling him to take her there—to take her there *now.* He chirped on and on until Wanda had to agree.

"Before we leave, I must tell my parents that I'm going," Wanda said. "We might be gone for days, and they will worry about me. I wouldn't want to cause them grief."

It is true that most of the time Wanda thought her parents weren't her real parents. And she often wished they would disappear. But sometimes, during lonely nights in the stillness of her bedroom, she thought they *could* actually be her parents. And even if they didn't show it with hugs and kisses or praise the way other parents did, they loved her deep down. This made the idea of her quest that much harder. But she summoned her determination, swept aside her uncertainty, and headed off to find them.

FIVE

Stay Away

Wanda heard her parents whispering in the kitchen. Were they planning a surprise for her birthday? Maybe this year they had remembered it. At the sound of their voices, Wanda's will to leave grew weak.

"I don't think I can do this," she said quietly to Voltaire, who was perched on her shoulder.

"You can and you must," he said. He pecked her head to urge her along, then took flight to meet up with her outside.

So Wanda entered the kitchen and told her parents that she was going off for a few days. Staying with a friend, she said, then waited to hear their protests, how this would ruin their birthday surprise.

"What a wonderful idea!" Her mother's face lit up.

"Yes, yes it is!" Her father wholly agreed. "In fact, that's just what we were discussing. This makes everything so much easier." Her parents shared a knowing look.

"Zane is so difficult," her father continued. "You see the way he is around you. You might be the cause of the problem here. So we were thinking that you should move out. Just for a while. Until he gets a little older." He smiled broadly.

"But I'll be gone for just a few days," Wanda said, growing dizzy. "I planned on coming back."

"Well, don't hurry, dear." Her mother patted her on the head. "Stay away as long as you can."

And with that, they ushered her through the back door and closed it firmly behind her.

Wanda stood in the yard next to a tall flowerpot filled with weeds. She gripped its rim, trying to steady herself. She took great gulps of air. It seemed that her birthday wish to be an orphan had finally come true.

"Well, it looks like you're ready!" Voltaire met Wanda in the yard. "Shall we go?"

"Yes," Wanda said. "Unfortunately, things turned out

better than I had expected." She told the bird what her parents had said.

"All the more reason to start this adventure," he chirped. "What luck, Wanda! No one will miss you!"

No one loves me, Wanda thought.

No one really cares about me.

No one cares what happens to me.

No one.

It was hard for Wanda to share Voltaire's good cheer with these thoughts circling around and around in her mind. But she tried. She took some fortifying breaths. She attempted to shake off the gloom that hugged her, and after a while, she did feel calmer. Soon her heart began to stir with optimism and hope. She went up to her room and quickly packed as much as her rucksack would hold; then the two headed off.

As Voltaire led her away from her home, she glanced back at the withered trees that framed the house. The once bright and welcoming front door was cracked and peeling, and the yellow shutters had turned grimy and gray. When had it all fallen apart? She couldn't say exactly. *Sometimes being close to a thing doesn't mean you can see it clearly,* she thought as she turned to the road again.

It was time to leave this dreary place behind.

It was time to find out the truth about her life.

SIX

The Scary Wood

Wanda and Voltaire stood at the edge of the forest.

They had traveled hours and hours to reach these woods, crossing meadows and valleys Wanda had never seen. Sometimes Voltaire flew just ahead of her, leading the way. Other times he perched on her shoulder, issuing orders.

"Turn left. Turn right. No, pardon me. That would be left, no, turn here, no, there, no, straight." His sense of direction was somewhat askew, and the way back to the woods took longer than either could have imagined. But as the sun began to set, they had reached their destination.

"Here we are. At last," Voltaire chirped. "Not to complain, your company is marvelous, really—except when you go all gloomy, that is—but flying alone is so much faster." He stretched his tired neck.

"Really," Wanda said with an arch of one eyebrow. Then she peered into the forest. She gazed up and up—over a hundred feet high—at the silvery gray trees that towered before her. Their leafy tops blocked out the remaining light of day.

She stepped between two of these giants, into their cool, dark shade, and shivered. "I'm not familiar with these woods. I've never traveled this way before."

"No need to worry. I am your guide." The bird flew a few feet ahead. "Just follow me. Into the Scary Wood."

"What? Wait! The Scary Wood? Why is it called the Scary Wood?"

"Because that's what it is. Smaller than a forest but more than a few trees. That's a wood."

"But why is it called the *Scary* Wood?" Wanda pressed.

"Because that's its name, dear girl. Come now, follow me. Into the Scary Wood we go. No need to be frightened. At least I don't think so."

Within two or three steps, they came to a fork in the path and stopped. Voltaire landed on Wanda's shoulder, trying to decide which way to turn.

Finally, he took off. "This way!" he called.

"Are you sure?" Wanda asked, hesitating.

"Not in the least," he answered. "But if we do not find anything pleasant, at least we shall find something new. So don't dawdle!"

Wanda shook her head. Should she follow or not?

She thought about her life back home. She couldn't go back there, at least not yet. And not just because her parents had told her to stay away. And not because she obviously didn't matter to them anymore—although this last reason would be reason enough.

No, it was something else.

For a long time now, she'd felt that something wasn't right. As if she'd been walking in a dream and couldn't see clearly. As if she'd been trying to look through blueberry jam.

She was determined to find out why. And something told her that this bird would lead her to the answers. She would have to summon all her courage and follow him into the unknown. Because one thing was certain— if there was a mystery to solve, she wouldn't find the answers at home.

"Wait up! I'm coming!" she called to the bird, who had flown out of sight.

In the few minutes that had passed, the air had grown chillier. The path had turned darker.

If we do not find anything pleasant, at least we shall find something new. Wanda shivered as she stepped onto the trail. She thought it strange that she knew nothing about these woods. But she would soon learn something very important about them. She would soon find out why no one *ever, ever* entered them.

SEVEN

Groods

"Does *any* of this look familiar?" Wanda stopped and slipped her rucksack off her shoulders. They ached from the weight of everything she had brought from home.

Voltaire settled close to her ear. It was night, although what time precisely, Wanda couldn't say. The air held a chill, but nothing more threatening. This part of the forest wasn't as dense, and the glow of the moon lit up the trees. Above, the sky was clear, with clusters of stars winking their arrival.

"Hmm." Voltaire nodded, looking at the branches above. "Ahhh," he said, gazing with intensity at the shrubs that surrounded them.

"Well?" said Wanda. Her eyes crossed in an effort to see the bird so close up. "Do you remember anything about the secret now?"

"Not a thing," he said.

Wanda frowned.

"I admit I am vexed by the lack of clues here," Voltaire said, flying up to the top of her head. "I was thoroughly convinced that a walk through the woods would jar my memory."

"So . . . what do you think we should do next?" Wanda asked.

"I suggest we stay right here and think for a spell," the bird said, fluffing his feathers, making himself comfortable. "Your hair has a lovely nest-like quality."

"We can rest for a while," Wanda agreed, "but could you please come down where I can see you?"

Wanda placed her rucksack against a tree, then sat on the ground and leaned against it. The bird hopped from her head to perch on her knee.

"Time to review," the bird said. "What do we know?"

Wanda was about to answer when she heard the crunch of a leaf. She gazed between the trees, but nothing unusual caught her eye.

Just the scurry of a forest animal, she thought.

Wanda scratched her head. "I don't think we know any more now than we knew an hour ago, or an hour before that, or an hour before that."

"Well said," Voltaire chirped, and Wanda sighed. At the end of her long breath, her ears picked up another sound. This time, the sharp snap of a twig.

"Did you hear that?" Wanda sat up straight, her whole body rigid.

"Yes." The bird nodded. "It's the sound of the woods. Night creatures, that's all."

Wanda slumped against the tree, relieved, and turned her attention back to their problem. *There must be something I can do or say to help him remember the secret.*

And then it came to her.

Why didn't I think of this before?

"Voltaire, I know you can't remember the secret, but can you remember who told it to you?"

"Well, of course I can," he said.

Wanda's eyebrows leaped up in surprise.

"I know, I know. You think I'm quite limited, with my small brain and all. Yes, Wanda, I heard you say it earlier, clear as a bell, but even though you believe—"

"Voltaire!" Wanda interrupted the bird. "Who told you the secret?"

"It was a lady."

"What lady—*AAAIII!*"

Wanda's rucksack was suddenly whipped out from behind her. She fell back and hit her head hard against the tree. And by the time she sat up, which was less than an instant later, she and Voltaire were surrounded.

Wanda tried to speak. But she could never have imagined the creatures that stood before her—no one could have—and she fell silent in fear.

There were at least ten of them of varying heights and heft, all dressed in rags. They were part human, part tree, part beast, and part bird.

The creature standing closest to Wanda stood at least six feet tall. Its arms and hands were covered in dark, craggy bark. On its head, leaves and green vines sprouted along with thick brown hair.

The beast to the left of it had a face covered in fur, with a nose shaped like a mushroom. On its right stood a very short creature with skin the texture of pinecones. Others had feathers. A few had skin that resembled the scales on bird legs.

If some were female and some were male, it would be impossible to say. Their clothes—torn pants, muddy shirts, shredded vests, ripped shoes—gave nothing away.

Any of this could have made Wanda's heart stop, but it was their eyes that kidnapped her breath. Cold eyes of stone, both vacant and menacing, stared at her.

"What do we have here?" said the tallest one, who had swiped her rucksack. Its voice was very deep. *This one's a male,* Wanda thought. He rifled through her bag, flinging things out as he noted each item.

"Shirt," he said, and Wanda watched as her favorite purple sweater landed in the shrubbery.

"Pants." These were caught by the short creature, who held them up like a coveted trophy. His face broke out in a lopsided grin, and Wanda saw that his rotted teeth were covered in moss.

"Book." With a flick of the wrist, Wanda's diary was hurled into the mud.

"STOP THAT!" Wanda couldn't help herself.

"Don't anger the Groods!" Voltaire whispered. "They're . . . unpredictable." Then he fluttered above her and tucked himself into the shadows of a branch overhead.

Groods? Wanda had never heard of such a thing. What were these creatures, exactly? Were they civilized or wild? They knew human words, but they had no manners at all.

She leaned forward to rescue her diary. Then she turned and snatched her sweater from the shrubbery beside her. "These things belong to me!"

The thieves broke out into laughter that was gruff and growly, surly and sour.

"Nothing belongs to you in the Scary Wood," the tall beast said. "In the Scary Wood, everything belongs to us." He stepped closer and leaned over her. "Including you." And with that, they trapped Wanda in a net made of rope and carried her away.

EIGHT

Let's Cook Her and Eat Her

"What if they cook me and eat me?" Wanda whispered to Voltaire, who had stowed away in her rope prison.

"Pure drivel," Voltaire whispered back as the Groods carried Wanda through the woods to their home. "They're gruesome, yes. To be feared, absolutely. But they're not cannibals. They don't eat humans."

"Let's cook her and eat her." The smallest creature kicked the net, jabbing Wanda in the ribs.

Voltaire's body stiffened. His head jerked up in surprise.

"We don't eat humans," the one with the mushroom nose said.

Voltaire relaxed. "Ah. That's better."

"But we could feed her to the bears. That might be fun."

"Oh, dear," the bird said, and he remained silent the rest of the journey.

When the Groods reached their home—a garbage-strewn campsite—they dumped the net on the ground, with Wanda still inside it. Voltaire flew to safety, hiding in a tangle of branches close by.

Wanda took in the details of the clearing. It was surrounded by trees and dotted with large boulders. A huge fallen trunk marked one of its boundaries.

She inhaled deeply to calm herself—and choked on the stench of rancid meat, the remains of past meals scattered about, circled by flies and swarming with maggots.

And then there was the Groods' bounty. Old, muddy backpacks in every color, large and small, piled higher than the tallest boulder. A variety of shoes and mismatched socks. Shredded jackets missing sleeves. Ragged pants missing legs. Torn books; old water bottles; pots and pans; a sleeping bag, slashed; a teddy bear, hacked to bits. And more. It all littered the forest floor.

What had happened to the children who owned these things? A shiver ran down Wanda's spine.

One of the Groods turned Wanda's rucksack upside down and shook it hard. Then the others pounced in a frenzy, grabbing, shoving, pulling, fighting for every piece.

Riiip. Off came a sleeve.

Yaaank. Pants split in two.

"Put those down!" Wanda yelled. "I need those clothes!"

Her shouts were ignored.

Buttons popped.

Collars and cuffs soared high in the air.

The woods echoed with the Groods' savage tug-of-war grunts.

It was clear to Wanda that this battle was for the sake only of claiming and destroying, and it made her heart race and her pulse pound.

Then, just as suddenly as the frenzy began, it ended, as if all at once they had become bored with the whole thing. The Groods drifted their separate ways except for one, who wandered over to Wanda.

"Beastly, wasn't it?" The Grood shook his head sadly.

"Yes." Wanda's voice came out in a whisper.

"A real pity," he said, turning to leave. "You're next."

"Voltaire!" Wanda called out to the bird after the Grood was a safe distance away.

Voltaire fluttered to the ground.

"Did you hear that? We have to escape—now." Wanda pulled hard at the net, trying to tear a hole in it. She tugged and tugged, but the rope was too strong. Her hands turned red in the struggle as the rope burned her palms.

"Yes. Escape. Not to worry. I've been devising a plan for that very thing," Voltaire said. "As I see it, we can accomplish this in two simple steps."

"Great!" Wanda said, rubbing her raw fingers. "What are they?"

"To escape," Voltaire said, "the first thing we must do is free you from the net. The second is to run."

I'm doomed, Wanda thought.

And she was right for more reasons than she knew, because just then the tallest of the beasts, the one with bark for skin, stomped toward her.

"Who were you talking to?" the Grood demanded, gazing about for the source of the other voice.

Given her circumstances, Wanda thought it would be best not to anger the creature, so she answered quickly and in a most straightforward manner.

"I was talking to this bird," she said, pointing to Voltaire.

"It is not wise to taunt me. Birds can't speak." The

beast's voice boomed. "WHO . . . WERE . . . YOU . . . TALKING . . . TO?"

"I don't mean to anger you," Wanda said in her sweetest voice. "Truly, I was talking to this bird."

The Grood's fury brought one of the other creatures scampering close, curious to see what the commotion was about. He was nearly Wanda's height, smaller than all the others—shorter than the shortest one she had seen earlier. The skin on his body looked like human skin, but hairier. His face had fuzzy cheeks, a small mouth, and a nose that resembled the nose of a deer.

Wanda might have gone so far as to say he was cute— for a Grood, of course. But his stony-eyed gaze crushed any kind thoughts.

The tall beast bowed at the waist, practically bending in half. He leaned so close to Wanda she could inhale his breath. It smelled like damp earth and wet leaves, more woodsy than human, and it made Wanda jerk back and shudder.

"Do you know what we do with troublemakers?" The tall Grood lowered his voice to a most-menacing timbre.

Wanda shook her head no.

"We slice 'em up." His cold rock eyes remained fixed

and unblinking. Wanda's temples began to throb under their stare.

"She looks like a nice person," the littlest one said in a high-pitched voice similar to Wanda's.

This creature is a girl, Wanda realized.

The female Grood gave Wanda an encouraging smile.

"I am. Really. I *am* a very nice person," Wanda tried to assure them.

The tall Grood snickered. "A nice person. We like nice people, don't we, Kitten?" he said to the little Grood, who nodded with enthusiasm.

Kitten? Really? Wanda stared at the little Grood's cold eyes and fang-like teeth.

"The nice ones—we slice 'em up extra thin. More to go around that way."

"That's what we do! That's what we do!" Kitten agreed.

"Now—who were you talking to?" the big Grood asked Wanda once again.

"I was talking to this bird. I mean no disrespect." Wanda turned to Voltaire. "Tell them, Voltaire. Tell them that I was talking to you."

Voltaire's head cocked to one side, then to the other. He gazed up into the giant's face, opened his beak, and—tweeted. *Tweet. Tweet. Tweet.* Then he spread his little blue wings and flew to a distant tree.

Wanda was stunned, but there was no time to dwell on what had just happened. The tall Grood lifted her, net and all, and raised her high in the air. Then he shook her with great cruelty and force.

Her arms and legs flew every which way. Her head bobbed and jerked. There was no doubt he would soon shake Wanda's skin from her bones.

But suddenly, he stopped. And grunted. And dropped her back to the ground.

"It's late," he said. "I'm tired. It's time for bed. I think I'll kill you at sunrise, when I feel more refreshed. It's such a treat to tear people limb from limb first thing in the morning."

"Yes! Yes!" cried Kitten, clapping her hands with delight. "We'll pull her completely apart in the morning!"

While Wanda tried to calm her thumping heart, each of the Groods lay down on the grass and fell asleep. Soon the clearing echoed with their groans, grumbles, and snores.

Wanda curled up in her rope prison, wishing her head would stop spinning. She could not fathom why Voltaire had behaved this way. He was her one and only friend, and he had betrayed her. She waited for him to return and explain. She waited and waited. But he never came back.

When the dizziness passed, she sat up to think. *What should I do now?* She shivered in the chilly night air.

She saw her favorite purple sweater snagged on a nearby shrub. She reached out, pulled it into her net, and raised it to her cheek. Its softness soothed her jagged spirit.

Then she put her mind to work. How would she escape? Just before she drifted off into a restless sleep, the answer became clear.

NINE

A Very Sharp Knife

"*Psst!* Kitten!"

It was just before dawn when Wanda called out to the smallest Grood.

The darkness of night was beginning to lift, but the clearing was still sheltered by shadow. Wanda could tell that the Groods would soon be awake—their snores had gone from deep rumbles to light snorts. It was important that Wanda talk to Kitten before they woke up.

"Kitten!" Wanda called out again. . . .

And the small Grood stirred. She placed a hairy hand over her ear as if to block Wanda's voice.

"Kitten!" Wanda tried once more.

"What?!" The little Grood sprang up. Her gaze traveled the campsite to see who had annoyed her.

"Over here," Wanda whispered.

The Grood stood and approached Wanda with great curiosity.

"My arms and legs have gone numb in this net." Wanda grimaced. "A small favor. Could you please cut me free—just so I can stretch?" Wanda asked. "If you could, I have something very special for you."

The Grood cocked her head, considering Wanda's offer. "What do you have?"

Wanda held up her favorite purple sweater. "I would give this to you—it's very silky and soft. I'm sure the others would like it, too. But you wouldn't have to fight for it. It would be all yours."

The Grood pursed her small lips, then nodded in agreement. "I'll be right back."

Wanda grew anxious as she waited for Kitten to return. What was taking her so long? Had the little Grood gone to wake her leader? The sky was growing lighter. The sun would soon rise. The other Groods began to twist and turn. They were nearing the end of their sleep.

Finally, Kitten came into view. She was alone and Wanda was relieved—until she saw what Kitten was

holding. She was grinning and gripping a knife. A very large, very sharp knife.

And what was that crusted on the tip of the blade?

It looked like dried blood.

Wanda's relief quickly turned to fear.

What had made her think she could trust this little Grood? She chided herself for a plan that now seemed not only foolish but fatal.

Kitten held out the knife.

Wanda held her breath.

Kitten jabbed the knife forward—and Wanda gasped. But the Grood began to saw away at the thick rope. She was astonishingly strong, and Wanda was quickly freed.

"Thank you." Wanda offered her the purple sweater, and the young Grood snatched it. Wanda wasn't surprised. The grimy shirt the girl wore had holes and tears, and the color had become impossible to tell. It was probably the same shirt she'd worn every day last week, last month, last year.

Wanda watched for her to put the sweater on, but instead, with a loud shriek, the little Grood joyfully set to ripping it to shreds.

Wanda was so startled by this that she forgot to flee. And by the time she did remember, the other Groods were awake.

One of them jumped up and shouted, "Get her!"

Wanda turned to run.

"Wait!" Kitten cried, grabbing her arm. "I want your hair, too." She lashed out with her knife, slicing an inch off Wanda's mane.

Wanda charged out of the clearing.

The ground vibrated with pounding Grood footsteps. She could hear their grunts as they chased her.

She ran and ran without direction or plan. But in this instance, she had something more important than strategy. She had luck.

Because, as Groods often do, they grew bored with the hunt. They slogged back to their clearing with the fresh hope that they'd find something already dead to rip to shreds.

When Wanda was confident that she was safe, she collapsed against the nearest tree. A cool, heavy fog hung over the forest, and Wanda shivered as she tried to catch her breath.

"Ah. Very good. Escape accomplished in two easy steps," a voice chirped overhead. "Just as I said. Simple, really. Just required some good common sense, I'd wager."

Voltaire had returned.

TEN

A Breeze Most Foul

"Voltaire! What happened to you? Why did you fly off?" Wanda leaped up to face the bird. "How could you leave me that way?"

How strange it is to feel both happy and angry at the sight of him, she thought. And it was even stranger, she realized, that her lips could smile while her fists were clenched at her sides.

"I went to seek help," Voltaire began to explain.

"But why wouldn't you speak to the Grood?" Wanda pressed. "Your silence put me in great danger."

"I am many things, Wanda, but I'm no match for Groods. You saw how wild and unpredictable they are.

A talking bird? Mangled in minutes, I'd say. Then just feathers and bone. No good to anyone, especially you."

Wanda's anger softened a bit. It was true that the Groods were unstable and nasty. She shuddered at the thought of them.

Voltaire fluttered down and landed on her shoulder. "I took to the trees, searching for someone to assist us," he went on. "No easy task in the Scary Wood, I might add."

Wanda's anger lightened a bit more.

"Then I heard Grood footsteps. Thundering footsteps. What a fright!" His blue head bobbed as he spoke. "But here you are. And now I must say, I am relieved and delighted to see that you're safe."

Wanda had to admit it all made sense, and her feelings of betrayal began to dissolve in the morning mist. And yet some doubt lingered.

"Voltaire, I'm sorry to say that I still don't know if I can rely on you."

"Well," he answered, "'the best way to find out if you can trust somebody is to trust them.'"

Hmm. Wanda thought about that. It seemed logical and wise. "Is that a quote from Voltaire? The writer, I mean."

"Dear girl, how many times must I tell you? I *am*

Voltaire. But if I quoted only myself, I'd be quite a bore. No, that was from Hemingway, another writer of some talent, I've heard."

Well, anyone who could quote the great writer Hemingway definitely deserved another chance, Wanda concluded. She decided to trust the bird. In less than two days, she had grown very attached to him, and she couldn't imagine their friendship ending.

Her faith in Voltaire mended, the two took off . . . and that's when Wanda remembered why they were there at all.

"Wait!" she said. "The secret. We were getting closer to unraveling this mystery. And then those horrible Groods showed up."

"Yes! That's right!" Voltaire said, hopping into the palm of Wanda's outstretched hand.

"Who did you say told you the secret?"

"It was the lady," he said.

"Which lady?" Wanda stopped and gazed into Voltaire's eyes, hoping to get him to focus.

"How odd," he said. "I can't seem to recall a thing about her."

"Concentrate. Close your eyes and try to imagine her," Wanda suggested.

Voltaire did as she asked. "I've got it!" he said.

"Who is she?" Wanda was very excited now. "Who is the lady?"

"I don't know! But I think we're meant to go to the top of a mountain. To a cave. Yes. No. Hold on. Not a cave. It's a castle. No, it's a cave. It's coming back to me. Slowly."

This wasn't what Wanda expected to hear, but it was a clue, and for that she was grateful and thrilled.

Voltaire tried to remember more. He tried very hard, but nothing else came to mind. So the two decided to take an uphill path to the mountaintop, where they would search for a cave.

Along the way, Voltaire settled in the crook of her arm, and they talked about all sorts of things. . . .

"Were you always able to speak?" Wanda asked.

"Yes," he said. "I can't remember a time when I couldn't."

"Of course you can't. You don't remember much." Wanda laughed.

"Where are your friends? Doesn't anybody like you?" he volleyed.

"Why do you think you're the writer Voltaire?" she shot back, which riled the bird, as she knew it would.

"I don't know why you insist I am not who I say I am. You are most difficult when it comes to this point."

Voltaire ruffled his feathers. "I am me. Voltaire. And quite pleased about it."

Wanda admired the bird's self-confidence. Sometimes she wished she were a different person. A person who shined. A person she could feel quite pleased about, too. Usually, she was able to dull the sharp edges of these thoughts. *Everyone has self-doubts,* she would tell herself, which was true enough and somewhat soothing. Now, though, after her parents had cast her out, she felt slight and small and hobbled.

Wanda had never shared these self-doubts with anyone, and she didn't want to share them with the bird. But she wasn't one to wallow in self-pity. She was quite the opposite, in fact. So right then, she came to a sudden decision. *I will show my parents that I count. Somehow, someday, I will prove to them that they were wrong to treat me so poorly. I am SOMEBODY, and I will make them see it.*

With this settled, Wanda turned her attention back to the bird. "If you are Voltaire, tell me, what have you written?"

"Wanda, dear, have you lost your senses? Birds do not write. My talent is to dispense wise thoughts to those in need." He gave Wanda a pointed look.

Wanda decided to abandon this argument. Voltaire did seem wise, and she wanted to seek his opinion on a nagging matter. It would mean sharing a secret with him. A secret she had never revealed to anyone before.

"All right, then," she said. "There's something that's been puzzling me. I'm wondering if you could help me figure it out."

Voltaire puffed out his chest. "Certainly, Wanda!"

"Sometimes, I have visions," she told him.

"What kind of visions?" the bird asked.

"I see my house, my garden. There's a little girl, dressed in yellow from cap to shoes, happily running through the flower beds."

"Is the little girl you?" Voltaire asked.

"That's the puzzle," Wanda said. "I think she must be, but it isn't a time I actually remember. What do you make of it?"

"Hmm. Let me think." Voltaire's head bobbed from side to side. Then he gazed up at the sky. He looked like he was about to pluck the answer right out of the air. Finally he spoke.

"Unfortunately, I don't have a clue."

"Well, *that* isn't very helpful," Wanda said.

"Wanda, dear, how could I possibly know what happened in *your* past? Haven't you noticed that I have enough trouble remembering *mine*?" He flew up to Wanda's shoulder to avoid her glare.

They walked in silence for a while. After several minutes, their argument faded from Wanda's mind. Something new had taken its place. She kept peering behind her. Casting sideways glances.

"What's wrong?" Voltaire asked.

"I can't shake the feeling we're being watched."

Voltaire craned his neck in every direction. "There's no one else here."

Wanda stopped short.

"Over there," she whispered, "in the shrubs. I see eyes."

Voltaire peered where instructed. "I don't see anything," he replied. "No insult intended, really, but I think you must be imagining them."

But Wanda was certain she had seen them—two dark, blinking eyes.

Was it a Grood? Had one followed her trail?

Wanda and Voltaire walked a bit farther, and she felt someone staring each step of the way.

This would have been enough to set her nerves tingling, but then a breeze began to blow.

It picked up quite suddenly. As if on command.

As she peered through the trees, the breeze seemed almost visible. Touchable. It swirled between the leaves, winding its way directly to her. Warm and charged and foul.

And as it grew closer, it began calling to her.

Wanda. Wanda. Her name rode on its wave.

"Voltaire, do you hear that?" She shuddered. "A voice. It's calling me."

"Yes, I hear it," the bird said with a flap of his wings. "A man's voice."

Wanda. Wanda.

A whisper on the wind.

Wanda. Wanda.

Her name floated toward her.

Beckoning her.

Wanda. Wanda. Come this way.

ELEVEN

The Swamp Gnome

Wanda. Wanda. Come this way.

"That voice. It's so frightening." Wanda shivered in spite of the morning sun that had warmed up the woods. "Who's calling my name? Who knows me here?"

Voltaire flew up to a tree limb to peer into the distance. "Those are very good questions," he said. "We must follow the voice to find out."

"But it sounds so evil." Wanda shook her head. "No, I think you're wrong. We should stay far away from it."

"I'm sure we should follow it," Voltaire insisted. "That way," he said, pointing to a path going off to the left.

"I'm sure we should not," Wanda said, noticing that the bird suddenly looked a bit woozy.

"But it will lead us to the mountaintop," Voltaire said, now sounding as if he were in a trance.

"What makes you think that?" Wanda asked as a glazed look settled in the bird's eyes. "Voltaire, are you all right?"

"I do feel a bit odd," he admitted. "Somewhat light-headed."

Wanda hoped that all their bickering hadn't made the bird sick. After all, he was just a little thing, not really built to bear much stress.

"I do think this path will lead to the mountaintop," Voltaire spoke slowly. "Something deep inside me is telling me so. And listen ... whoever was calling your name has stopped. He's gone now."

Wanda still had a bad feeling about this path, but Voltaire had already taken flight, so she dashed after him. They moved through the trees, the bird fluttering just slightly ahead of her. From time to time, she thought she saw the blinking black eyes in the bushes they passed. But she couldn't be certain.

The forest was strangely quiet. No chirps. No rustling. No buzzing. Except for the soft patter of Voltaire's wings, no sounds at all.

It made Wanda wary, but the path began to lead uphill, and this gave her some hope that they were headed in the right direction.

As they continued on, the air became misty. Soon it turned into a gray fog that was difficult to see through. Even though Voltaire flew just ahead of her, she couldn't spot him anymore. And she wasn't sure, but she thought the path had started to go *down* again.

"Do you think we're still headed in the right direction?" she called out, but the bird didn't reply.

Finally, she came to the end of the path, where the fog had lifted slightly. Instead of finding a cave at the top of a mountain, she found herself standing at the edge of a swamp. "Oh, nooo!" she moaned.

Voltaire flew onto her shoulder.

The swamp water was thick and milky green. It surrounded the trees, and a white swirling smoke drifted up from its surface.

"We've made a mistake," Wanda said. "This swamp is too big and there's no way to cross it. We took the wrong path."

"You took the right path," a deep voice said from inside the smoke.

It was the same voice she had heard calling to her

before. "Where is he?" Wanda whispered to Voltaire. "Can you see who it is?"

But before the bird could answer, a figure stepped out of the swirling mist.

He was taller than a boy and shorter than a man, but he was neither.

His strange green skin matched the color of the swamp. His long pointy ears stood out from his bald, lumpy head. Around his middle he wore a brown tattered rag that hung like a skirt to his knobby knees. His round belly bulged over it.

"Who are you?" Wanda asked.

"I am the swamp goblin. I rule this bog," he replied. "Follow me." Then he smiled at Wanda, and his eyes glowed red. She leaped back at the sight of them.

Wanda started backing down the path. "Er, we'll just be going now. We've come the wrong way."

"No, you haven't. You're exactly where you should be," he said.

Then he reached out and touched Wanda's arm with a wet green hand—and she suddenly and completely disappeared.

TWELVE

Vanishing Wanda

Voltaire let out a shriek as Wanda disappeared right out from under him. He fluttered wildly to avoid hitting the ground.

"Voltaire!" Wanda called out. She saw his eyes dart about, searching for her. "This way!"

Wanda had reappeared in the middle of the swamp. She stood on a patch of land the size of a doormat. The goblin stood on it, too, still clutching her arm.

"Oh, there you are! That was quite a trick!" Voltaire said, mesmerized at her sudden vanishing. He hopped up and down at the swamp's edge. "This is excellent, Wanda! You may have discovered a new talent."

"Voltaire, I think I'm in trouble here," she said as the goblin grabbed her arm tighter.

"Yes, indeedy," the goblin said with glee. "You're in very big trouble! The finest kind." Then his free arm swept forward, and Wanda could see he was holding a cane. It was a stick of old wood, crooked and gnarled, with an image of his face crudely carved into its top.

He waved the cane over the swamp, and the swirling smoke began to take shape. It churned and twisted, forming figures of men and women, young and old.

As the hazy forms floated through the trees, more smoke rose from the water, turning into children, boys and girls of fog and mist.

With eyes and mouths opened wide in terror, they all cried out, "Help me! Who am I? Tell me my name!"

Wanda gasped at the horrifying sight.

"Welcome to Gravesend Landing." The goblin gave a short bow. "Your new home."

He tapped his cane on the ground, and Wanda felt a tingling in her arms and her hands. Then from the top of her head all the way down to her toes.

She gazed at her feet and cried out, "I can see right through them!" And it was true. Her shoes and feet had

turned to vapor, and she could see straight through to the ground they stood on.

She held up her hands and shuddered as the gauzy swamp sunlight set them aglow, inside and out.

In a wave of shock, she hugged herself tightly, and her breath caught in her throat. Her arms were as soft as cotton candy.

Every part of her had begun to fade. She started to feel lighter and lighter—until she felt as light as the air.

"Help me!" Her cry joined the others. "I—I'm disappearing!"

She faded and faded, and the more she did, the less she could remember. "Help me! Help me! I can't remember my name."

"Wanda!" Voltaire shouted to her. "You are Wanda!"

"Wanda! Wanda!" she repeated, and the tingling weakened, but it didn't stop.

"Keep at it, Wanda! Don't forget who you are!" Voltaire said.

"Wanda! Wanda!" she cried out. She yelled loud and strong and without pause. "Wanda! Wanda! Wanda! Wanda!" And the fading began to slow.

"That's it!" Voltaire cheered.

"I am Wanda Seasongood!" she shouted with great force. And with her last name declared, the fading halted.

"Wanda! Wanda! Wanda Seasongood!" she shouted again and again, but her name didn't hold the power she needed to reverse the goblin's magic. Her heart began to race in fright. She was still see-through, still a body of mist.

"Enough of this. It is time to join the others." The little man sneered and raised his cane. He aimed its carved head at Wanda. . . .

And a breeze began to blow.

It was warm and charged and foul—just like the breeze that had carried her name.

And it started to blow Wanda apart.

THIRTEEN

Have Courage!

"Help me! I'm breaking up!" Wanda cried as the breeze swirled around her.

"Don't forget who you are!" Voltaire called out. "Have courage!"

"I'm Wanda! I'm brave!"

"That's working! I think you're becoming more solid! Say more! Say more!"

"I'm smart and I'm careful!" Wanda shouted, and indeed she could feel herself growing a bit more substantial.

"Good! Good!" the bird cheered.

"I'm always polite!"

"No. Don't think so. You're fading again."

The breeze picked up and started blowing Wanda to pieces.

"I'm very kind!" she yelled in a panic.

"Uh, that doesn't appear to be true, either. You're going all ghosty. And your legs are drifting away."

Voltaire beat his wings frantically, trying to send Wanda's legs back to her.

"So touching." The goblin laughed at the sight. He sucked in a bucket of air and filled his cheeks to bursting. Then, with one mighty blow, he blasted Wanda again. Her arms blew away at the elbows. Her head bobbed in the wind.

"Oh, noooo!" Wanda wailed. But she took a moment to calm herself, then focused on remembering who she was.

"I'm thoughtful! I'm honest! I'm trustworthy!" she cried out.

"That's better! More! More!" Voltaire chirped.

"I can't sing! I have no friends!" Wanda yelled, and her limbs began to float back to her.

"Sad, but true," Voltaire agreed. "Go on! Go on!"

"I'm a good listener!"

"Hmm. Maybe not." Voltaire watched Wanda's ears drift away from her head.

"I'm loyal! Responsible! Hopeful!" Wanda shouted, and she could feel herself going from wispy to weighty.

"Yes! Yes! Yes!" Voltaire whooped with joy.

"No! No! No!" The swamp goblin stomped his feet. "I cannot allow this." He raised his arms and the air around Wanda churned and set her whirling—but she fought back hard.

She continued to shout every true thing she could say of herself . . .

And it worked.

She went from smoky to see-through and back to solid—and became Wanda again. And she was never happier to be who she was.

FOURTEEN

An Awful Screech

"Well done, Wanda!" Voltaire flew circles around her as she tested her arms and legs. She was a bit dizzy from the whirling and twirling, and it took a few moments for her head to stop spinning. But when it did, she became aware of an awful screech.

"What's that terrible sound?" Wanda's gaze traveled the swamp and came to rest on the goblin, who sat hunched on a rock a few feet away.

His piercing sobs echoed through the bog. Fat tears rolled down his cheeks and plopped into the folds of his skirt. "They all forget who they are without fail." He lifted his head to peer at Wanda. "And as soon as they do, they turn to smoke. Then they're trapped here at Gravesend Landing, and they belong to me. I've never lost one. Never ever. Until you."

Then his head dropped down, nearly touching his lap, and he wailed and wailed.

Wanda quickly looked around for the other ghost figures. Perhaps there was some way she could help them. But she saw in an instant that nothing could be done. They had scattered in the breeze, and the swamp air swirled once more with their smoky remains.

"Follow me," Wanda whispered to Voltaire as the goblin continued to howl. She leaped from stone to stone to the edge of the bog. Then she and Voltaire stepped through the trees and crept silently away.

Wanda was proud of her excellent escape. But her joy was mixed with confusion. She had always considered herself kind. So why, then, had she continued to disappear when she shouted it out?

I'm a nice person. I'm definitely a nice person, she thought, trying to console herself.

After all, no matter how unfairly her parents had treated her, hadn't she always been respectful and helpful? And no matter how horribly Zane had behaved, hadn't she always been nice to him? Had she ever struck back at him? Had she ever tried to get even? Never. Not once.

And just now—after she had escaped—wasn't her first thought to save the ghost people in the swamp? Weren't all of those signs of a kind person?

What was the unkind thing she had done?

Wanda was stumped.

FIFTEEN

The Key to the Secret

"Voltaire, I don't think I've ever been that frightened before." Wanda pinched her arm to make sure she was still solid. "I nearly disappeared."

"Yes! It was quite exciting. Dreadful, yet thrilling," he chirped.

"Evaporating is not thrilling." Wanda had recovered, but there was still a toll to pay for fading to smoke. Her arms felt rubbery and her legs were unsteady, and she moved through the forest with a definite wobble.

She walked through the woods slowly. And twice she glimpsed the blinking black eyes. Hidden in the shrubbery. Following her path. Each time she saw them, her chest tightened and a sharp pain of fear shot through her forehead.

But when the eyes didn't reappear a third time, she wondered if she had seen them at all. There and gone. There and gone. Was her mind playing tricks on her?

I'm still very shaken and on edge, Wanda thought. *I need to calm down. That must be the problem.*

"Let's sit," she suggested. "My legs feel like jelly."

They found a spot near a blueberry bush. Wanda and Voltaire were so famished, they immediately began to pick the berries. This was the perfect place to rest.

As they ate, they talked about the swamp goblin and Wanda's amazing escape. It was exhilarating to relive now that she was safe.

"You know," Wanda said, "it's very disturbing to think I'm unkind."

"Yes, that was baffling." Voltaire pecked at a berry. "After all, you seem nice. Well, nice enough."

"I *am* nice," Wanda insisted. "And I can't imagine why anyone would think . . ."

And then it came to her.

"Oh, noooo," she moaned. "Voltaire, I *have* been unkind! Actually, I've been very, very mean."

Then she told Voltaire about her birthday wishes.

"It's a very bad thing, hoping your brother and parents disappear. But I've wished it year after year. And now that I've actually disappeared myself, I know how terrible it is. It's terrifying. No, I'll never make that wish again."

"Hold on! Did you say something about a brother?"

"Yes, I have a brother. He's repulsive and nasty. Like a pig and a mole and a snake all in one. But I will no longer wish him harm."

"That's it! That's it!" Voltaire's wings beat in a flapping fit. "I remember the secret! I remember it!"

"Really?" Wanda said, forcing herself to remain composed. She'd been down this path of false hope before.

"It's about a brother! Your brother is being held captive in the Scary Wood."

Wanda jumped up. "I knew it! I knew it! I knew there was a secret in my family. All that hunting and prying and snooping—and at last I have discovered it. I can hardly believe it—I have another brother!"

Voltaire was quite pleased with himself. "Once you free your brother, you will know the truth about your life! Your brother is the key."

The secret she finally found was all too much. Wanda grabbed on to a tree, trying to catch her breath. Finally,

finally, she possessed the clue she'd been searching for—the clue that might change her life forever.

Wanda's spirit soared to the sky and circled the sun. "Thank you, Voltaire! Thank you so much!" She kissed the bird on the crest of his head.

I will find my brother and bring him home, Wanda thought. *And my parents will finally respect me. I will rescue him, and they will see how wrong they were to toss me out so easily.*

"I have another brother!" Wanda was beside herself with the news and filled to the top with questions. *What's he like? Does he know about me? Do we resemble each other? Why is he in the woods?* she wondered.

"Voltaire, can you tell me who is holding my brother? And why?"

"Hmm. That's a tough one." Voltaire thought very hard. "Well, I don't know," he concluded. "But I might have known it once. So there's hope that I'll know it again."

"Where do you think we should look for him?" Wanda asked. "We must find him. Let's start right now!"

"Where should we look? Where should we look?" Voltaire paced the ground, head down, pecking at blueberries while he thought.

"I know!" His head jerked up, a blueberry stuck to the

top half of his beak. "In the cave. That must be it. He must be in the cave."

"The cave. Of course!" Wanda said. "But there are so many paths in the Scary Wood. And there's so much danger here. How will we stay alive to find it?"

Wanda stared off, mulling over the problem—when a pair of eyes appeared in the nearby shrub.

Blinking black eyes.

They disappeared. Then they came back again. This time nearer, because whoever it was had moved closer.

They blinked again. And came closer still.

"Voltaire, look," Wanda whispered. "The eyes."

Blink.

Closer.

Blink.

Still closer.

Then a voice.

Eyes and a voice.

"I know where the cave is," the voice said. "I'll tell you where it is."

SIXTEEN

Prince Frog

With another blink, the mystery figure leaped from the shrubbery and landed precisely before them.

"You're a frog!" Wanda said. "And you talk, too!"

"You're a genius," the frog replied. "Very sharp of you to notice."

That's all it took for Wanda to form an instant dislike for the frog.

"You've been following us for hours," Wanda said. "You nearly scared me to death, stalking us that way. That wasn't very nice. What do you want?"

"You're my princess," the frog said. "I want a kiss. Kiss me."

"Ha! That's not likely to happen," she said. Wanda had never met a creature so bold and so irritating. And that would have been enough by itself to make her refuse his kiss. But there was something else. Wanda liked fairy tales, but she did not believe for one moment that a kiss could turn any frog, even one that could talk, into a prince. She was not about to be tricked.

"Just one kiss," the frog said. "One kiss will be all that it takes. Kiss me."

She looked at the frog's green slimy skin. His bulgy black eyes. His big froggy mouth. And the issue was settled. "No. I would never kiss a frog."

"But I know the cave you're searching for." The frog gave a sly grin. "Kiss me and I'll tell you where it is. Kiss me. Kiss me."

More than anything, Wanda wanted to find her brother. But her glance settled on the frog's mucousy skin, and she couldn't bear the thought of a kiss, not even one. "No, I cannot kiss you."

"Just one kiss!" he cried with a wide-open jaw, and a glob of frog spit flew from his mouth.

"Yuck! No!"

"Kiss me. Kiss me. Kiss me."

"Never. Never. Never."

"If I may interrupt . . ." Voltaire entered the fray.

"Wanda, a word, please." Voltaire turned to the frog. "Would you excuse us, sir?"

"Sure." The frog shrugged. "She's my one true love. I can wait."

"Perhaps just one kiss," Voltaire suggested to Wanda. "It might prove to be helpful."

"I won't kiss a frog. Especially that one."

"But he really might know where the cave is," Voltaire said, trying to persuade her.

"Then *you* kiss him." Wanda shook her head.

"Please, just think about it. . . ."

Then, at that moment, they both looked at the frog, and it was exactly the wrong moment because—WHAP!—the frog flicked out his tongue, caught a fly, and gulped it down. "Ahh. Delish." He burped, then grinned at Wanda. "Kiss me."

"Would you kiss that?" Wanda shook her head. "No," she answered for Voltaire. "But I have an idea."

They returned to the frog, and Wanda smiled sweetly, hoping to charm him into helping them.

"My name is Wanda," she said in her friendliest voice.

"I am the royal Prince Frog," the frog replied.

"The royal Prince Frog?" Wanda said. "That doesn't sound right. Don't you mean the royal Frog Prince?"

"I know who I am," the frog said. "You're very difficult. But you're still my princess. Kiss me. KISS ME. KISS ME. KISS ME. KISS ME. KISS

ME. KISS ME. KISS ME. KISS ME. KISS ME. KISS ME. KISS ME. KISS ME. KISS ME."

"ABSOLUTELY NOT."

"Well then, I won't tell you which path to take. You will never find the cave."

"We will find it on our own," Wanda said in a huff. She turned to the bird. "Which way, Voltaire?"

Voltaire studied the paths. There were three, and it looked like he had no idea which one to choose. But then his eyes glazed over. And when they cleared again, he pointed. "This way."

He hopped onto Wanda's shoulder and they started off.

"Wrong. Wrong. Wrong," the frog said. "Kiss me, and I'll set you straight."

Wanda and Voltaire ignored the frog and continued on their way.

"Kiss me. Kiss me. Kiss me." They could hear the frog croaking even at a distance. But Wanda had made up her mind. She would find her brother on her own and there would be no kiss.

The frog headed back into the shrubs. "If that's what you want," he grumbled. "But you're making a mistake. A big mistake." He slurped up another fly. "And, really, I wouldn't go that way if I were you. . . ."

SEVENTEEN

The Nixie

After walking for miles and getting nowhere, Wanda had second thoughts about the frog. "Maybe I *should* have kissed that slimy creature."

"'The course of true love never did run smooth,'" Voltaire chirped. "A quote from Shakespeare," he told Wanda before she could ask.

"True love? Really, Voltaire?" Wanda pictured the frog and laughed.

It was mid-afternoon, the sun was shining, and the woods buzzed with activity. Yellow and purple wildflowers grew alongside the path, with bees and butterflies darting among them. Wanda spotted a doe eating berries under the shade of a tree. Sweet birdsong filled the air, and somewhere nearby there was a stream—Wanda could hear the sounds of water splashing over rocks. The loveliness of it all made Wanda forget how frightful a place this was.

Wanda strayed off the path to find the stream. Then she and Voltaire walked along its shore. The flowing water glinted under the sunlight, and every now and then, they caught sight of a trout leaping into the air. So peaceful.

They followed the river to the end, where it flowed into a clear blue lake.

"This part of the Scary Wood looks so different," Wanda said. "Bright and open and fresh. And the water—I feel like it's calling to me."

She lowered her hand into the lake. It was warm and comforting. A sudden calm came over her and every muscle in her body relaxed. She hadn't realized how tense she was until now.

"This is magical," she said to Voltaire. "This water is so soothing."

She cupped her hand and filled it with water. She wanted to splash some on her face. But when she tried to lift her hand out of the water, she couldn't. She twisted

and turned. She grabbed her arm with her free hand and tugged. Nothing worked.

"Is there a problem?" Voltaire asked, observing Wanda's strange contortions.

"The lake has my hand and it won't give it back!" Wanda said, her calm replaced with alarm.

Then the center of the lake began to churn, and rising from the bubbling water, a woman appeared. She was the most beautiful creature Wanda had ever seen.

Her eyes matched the green of the lily pads. Her skin shimmered a silvery blue. When Wanda took a closer look she could see why. Her skin was made of the smallest scales, delicate and pearly.

Her silky blue hair hung down to her waist. Her arms and legs were long and elegant, with hands and feet that were slender and graceful. Webbing grew between her fingers and between her toes.

"Who are you?" Wanda asked, mesmerized.

"I am a nixie, a water spirit," she replied, her voice as light as a raindrop.

"Are you holding me here?" Wanda asked, still unable to pull her arm out of the water.

"I am *helping* you," she said. "There's no need to

struggle. Come with me beneath the water, where there is no misery and despair."

"I am not miserable. Really," Wanda said, her heart beginning to thump with fear. "And I'm not in despair. I'm fine. I'm totally fine. Please let me go."

"But you're not fine," the nixie said. "You're not fine at all."

The nixie rose above the water. Surrounded by a pearly blue mist, she drifted through the air to stand next to Wanda. Her eyes met Wanda's—and with only her glance, she robbed Wanda of her will. Then she filled her with anguish.

Wanda's thoughts turned dark with woe: *Life is too hard. There is no point in trying. Nothing gets better. Things only get worse.*

All at once, Wanda was overcome with sorrow and grief and bleakness and gloom.

She thought about finding her brother—and now expected that she would fail in her quest. They would never find the cave. Or leave here alive. She wouldn't be able to prove to her parents that they'd been wrong to treat her so badly. They would never offer the apology that she deserved to hear.

The nixie touched her shoulder, and Wanda felt every bit of joy drain from her. Her spirit sunk to the darkest depths, and her body felt foreign to her, like an empty vessel.

With all hope gone, she mourned everything that would never come to pass. No brother. No wishes. No dreams. No possibilities at all. The pain of it was too much to endure—and she began to cry.

Her eyes filled with tears that streamed down her face. Tears poured from her skin. Her shoes filled with puddles. Her clothes became drenched in her sadness.

"Leave her alone!" Voltaire squawked at the nixie.

"She's mine now." The nixie laughed, revealing sharp, pointy teeth. She was a hideous creature under false beauty.

"Voltaire, I'm feeling so lost and so weak." Wanda tried to break free of the nixie's grip. She tried to fill her mind with happy, hopeful thoughts.

And it was beginning to work. For an instant, Wanda felt the nixie's power weaken. Then it took hold again, and Wanda felt something else. A squishy feeling in her feet. She tried to look down, but she was frozen in the nixie's spell.

"Voltaire! My feet—they feel strange. I think they're dissolving. Or wait—no. I think she's trying to turn me into a mermaid. I don't want to be a mermaid!"

Voltaire gazed down. "No worries there. She's not turning you into a mermaid."

Wanda felt some relief. "Thank goodness. I wouldn't want to lose my legs!"

"Your legs are still there—and you'll have so many more," he told her. "She's turning you into a squid."

EIGHTEEN

Pucker Up

"A squid?! I don't want to be a squid!" Wanda wailed. "Somebody help me!"

A tentacle wriggled out of Wanda's left knee. Another burst from her right one.

"Help! Help!" she cried out.

"Hello, Princess. Did I hear you calling for help?"

"Oh, noooo! Not you!" At the sight of the frog, Wanda's distress doubled in size.

"Princess, I tried to warn you. 'Wrong path,' I said. Did you listen? No." The frog shook his head. "And now look—you have tentacles, and they're sprouting little suction cups. Very attractive."

"Suction cups!" Wanda moaned. "No! No! No!"

SUSAN LURIE

"Frog, be gone." The nixie sneered. "You're disturbing my concentration. I must focus now to capture this girl for the lake."

"But you'll surely kill her," Voltaire said. "A squid needs the ocean."

"And why would I care about that?" the nixie replied. "I simply want to turn this girl into a squid."

Wanda felt her foot disappear—and three arms grow in its place. "Voltaire, my foot is gone—and my head is growing larger!" Wanda's voice quivered with fear.

"It's not very practical," Voltaire said to the nixie. "A squid cannot survive in a lake."

"Voltaire, I think my head is going flat. Somebody, help me!"

"Kiss me and your troubles will be over, Princess. Kiss me. Kiss me."

"Voltaire! At least tell this frog to GO AWAY!"

"You two are distracting me." The nixie turned to the frog and the bird. "I think I'll change you both into guppies."

"Wanda," Voltaire whispered in her ear, "you must kiss the frog. It's our last hope. He might turn into a human, and then he could help us."

Wanda felt her tentacles writhing, and though she

hated to admit it, kissing the frog was the only sensible thing to do.

"All right, frog. Come here." She took a deep breath. "I'll kiss you."

The frog leaped up.

The nixie swung at him to swat him away. The frog was too quick, and she missed.

He puckered his lips.

Wanda closed her eyes as he reached her mouth.

His lips were cold and wet and slimy.

With a loud *smack*, they kissed. Then the frog landed on the ground next to Wanda's remaining foot.

They stared deeply into each other's eyes.

And waited in silence.

Even the nixie watched to see what would happen next.

They waited.

And waited.

And waited.

And nothing happened.

"*Ack!*" said the frog. "It didn't work. How disappointing. You're still a girl."

NINETEEN

Phfft!

The nixie laughed. "You are all so foolish."

Although the kiss had been an out-and-out failure, it still proved to be helpful. While the nixie had been watching, her magic had slipped. Wanda noticed that her tentacles had started to shrink, and her foot had quickly grown back. And suddenly she knew how to escape the nixie—they had to distract her!

"Frog!" she whispered. "I need your help. Kiss the nixie!"

The frog turned to the nixie at once. "Kiss me. Kiss me." He puckered his lips. "Kiss me! Kiss me! Kiss me!"

"Go away, you pest!" She swiped at the frog, forgetting

about Wanda for just a moment—but that was all that it took.

Wanda's hand came free of the lake. She yanked it hard—and it flew out. But it flew with such force that she lost her balance and fell into the water.

SPLASH!

The nixie spun and let out a shriek. "My hex on the lake has been broken! Look at me, girl!" She tried to recapture Wanda in a spell.

"Don't look! Don't look!" croaked the frog. "Run!"

Wanda took off. Voltaire soared by her side. The two moved as fast as they could. They ran into the woods, but soon their chests burned with fatigue. Panting, they stopped to rest behind a large tree.

"That frog turned out to be much better than a prince," Wanda said between gasps. "He saved my life."

"Indeed," Voltaire wheezed from a branch above.

"I think I should follow *him* from now on!" Wanda bent down to tie her shoe. "Because you seem to deliver me into all kinds of trouble. Groods. A goblin. A nixie. I've nearly lost my life three times."

Hmm. That set Wanda to thinking. *Was it strange that Voltaire's choices were all bad ones?*

"I wonder, Voltaire, if I should continue on my own? Can I really trust you?"

The words flew out of her mouth before she could consider them. And by the time her lace was tied and she had straightened up, Voltaire had spread his wings and flown away.

"Voltaire! Wait!" Wanda cried out, but the bird didn't reply. "Well, fine. Just leave. I can do this on my own." Wanda was shocked by Voltaire's hasty departure. And if truth be told, she was hurt, too. As she considered what to do next, a silvery blue mist formed in the air. The pearly haze could mean only one thing: The nixie had followed her.

Wanda ran.

"I will find you!" The nixie's shrill cry chased her through the forest.

Wanda raced through the trees in terror. She took twists and turns, then doubled back, then changed direction again, trying to lose the dreadful creature. In a frenzy, she left the trail altogether, leaped over logs, crawled beneath shrubs, and finally found herself in a darker part of the forest.

The trees looked very different here. They were all short and blackened, as if their crowns had been scorched.

And the ground was bare. No grass grew. No flowers. Not even weeds.

Heart pounding, Wanda stopped. She had come to a bridge that hung over a river. She couldn't tell how deep the water was. The bridge was rickety, the kind made of vines and planks, and it swung wildly in the breeze.

This bridge is dangerous, but the nixie is worse, Wanda thought. *I must try to cross it.* She grabbed its rope railing to steady herself—and a mouse scampered through her legs.

"Ohhh!" Wanda jumped in surprise.

The mouse dashed across the creaky planks, and when it reached the center of the bridge—*Phfft!*—it exploded in a small puff of smoke.

Wanda didn't trust her eyes. Had that really happened? She had nearly convinced herself that it hadn't, when she spotted a squirrel. It stood on the other side of the bridge. It waved its tail at Wanda. It twitched its cute nose. Then it scampered toward her. When it reached halfway—*Phfft!*—a flame shot up out of nowhere and roasted the creature. It disappeared in a cloud of gray.

"How awful!" Wanda leaped off the bridge and back onto the riverbank.

The mist had turned to a light blue rain, and Wanda was thoroughly drenched in it. She listened for the nixie's cries—they were growing louder and closer.

Wanda looked under the bridge, planning to swim beneath it. *I'll follow that duck paddling there,* she thought.

She took a step toward the water, and—*Phfft!* As the duck passed under the bridge, it was blasted to bits. Its soft downy feathers hung in the air, then blew away in the breeze.

Wanda trembled in shock. Clearly, there was no way to cross this river. And there was no going back the way she came, either, with the nixie chasing her. She was trapped.

"This way!" A girl's voice cut through her fear. It was Kitten, the Grood. She stood on the other side of the creek, waving Wanda over.

"I can't cross the bridge. I'll explode."

"No, you won't! You can cross!" Kitten said. "You are covered in pearly blue mist. It will keep you safe."

Was the Grood telling the truth? Why would she want to help?

"Wanda!" The nixie broke through the trees.

"Hurry!" the Grood called. "She can't cross the bridge. She can't stray that far from the lake."

"I've got you!" The nixie reached out with her long webbed hand, grabbing for Wanda.

Wanda looked at the nixie.

She looked at the Grood.

She looked at the bridge.

All bad choices.

All right, she thought. *Which way should I die?*

TWENTY

Sizzle and Steam

"Wanda, you're mine!" The nixie's long fingers caught Wanda's sleeve in a pinch. Wanda's heart skipped as she twisted away.

"Do not cross that river." The nixie gurgled and spat. "You belong to me. You belong to the lake."

"Hurry! Hurry!" The Grood waved to Wanda. "Cross the bridge now!" She jumped up and down, trying to convince Wanda that there was no time to spare.

Wanda stepped onto the bridge again. She checked her arms and her legs, her head and her feet. She was still covered in the pearly blue mist. Would it really keep her from exploding?

Wanda's hands trembled as she grabbed hold of the

bridge's rope railing. Then she slowly placed a foot on a plank.

The bridge swung and dipped, and Wanda careened wildly, first left, then right. She gasped and waited for it to stop lurching, but the Grood was shouting, "Keep going! Keep going!" so she took another step.

"No! Stop! You'll explode!" the nixie cried out.

Wanda turned to the nixie. Her green eyes glowed a fiery orange, and Wanda's heart fluttered with fear. She stepped onto the next plank.

"That's it!" the Grood shouted. Her lips curled in a menacing smile. The fuzz on her cheeks stood on end. Her nostrils twitched with an air of excitement, as if she was already imagining the horrible things she would do to Wanda, her splendid prize.

I will make it to the other side, and then I'll reason with the Grood, Wanda thought. *I'll convince her not to tear me to shreds. Yes, that's exactly what I'll do, and all will be well.*

Wanda took another step on the bridge and another. And then a bunny streaked across her path. She froze as it started over the bridge. In the middle of the bridge, it stopped.

Wanda's breath caught in her throat as she watched the bunny glance about. It sniffed at the air with its little pink nose. It lifted a foot and scratched an ear. Wanda

sighed with relief. The rabbit was fine. Did that mean she would be, too?

The bunny hopped to the next plank—and its fluffy white cotton tail burst into flames.

"Oh, noooo!" Wanda cried as the animal was blasted from sight.

"Don't be afraid!" the Grood called. "The pearly blue mist will protect you, I promise. Keep going!"

Small beads of sweat dotted Wanda's forehead. There was nothing to do but continue. She took one more step, then another. She swallowed a great gulp of air—and stepped on the plank where the bunny had blown up.

She struggled to breathe as the wood sizzled and steamed under her foot.

But she did not explode.

Another step. Sizzle. Another step. Steam. Step after step, sizzle and steam. She walked faster and faster, sparks flying as she lifted her heels.

The bridge lurched and swayed under her weight—but she was close to the end now. She broke into a run—and red embers burned under the soles of her shoes.

As she reached the far side, the nixie howled a long wail of defeat.

Breathless, Wanda took one final leap off the bridge—and nearly landed right in the arms of the waiting Grood.

"See! I told you!" The Grood nodded happily at Wanda's success. "You did it! You crossed the bridge. You're alive!"

The Groods were not Wanda's friends, but Wanda knew what had to be said. "Thank you, Kitten. Thank you so much. You saved my life."

The Grood shrugged, as if saving people was what she naturally did.

The sun was setting over the woods. The two girls stood in its gentle glow and peered down the bridge. On the other side, the nixie was melting into a pearly blue puddle.

"That's what she does whenever she loses." Kitten smiled and laughed. Then she gazed up at Wanda—and stared at her with her cold stone eyes.

"You crossed the bridge," she said, her smile slowly collapsing into a sneer. "Now it's time to pay the toll."

TWENTY-ONE

Follow the Bunchberries

"The toll? What toll?" Wanda asked, taking a giant step back.

"Your purple sweater was very nice," the Grood said, eyeing Wanda's shirt. "I want more clothes."

"But you already have all my clothes," Wanda said. "That tall Grood took my rucksack with everything in it. You have all my possessions. These are the only clothes I have left." Wanda pointed to what she was wearing.

"That's what I want! That's what I want!" The Grood nodded. "I want what you're wearing."

"That's impossible. I will not walk through the forest naked," Wanda said, shocked at the notion.

"Then give me your eyeglasses. I want to break them apart and shatter them to pieces."

"I will not give you my glasses." Wanda reached up to make sure they sat securely on her nose. "I can't see without them."

"Well, it's not fair." The Grood jammed a hand into her pocket and pulled out a pair of very sharp scissors. "I helped you cross the bridge. Now you have to pay the toll. I want a prize."

"The biggest reward for a thing well done is to have done it," a voice called out.

"Who said that?" the Grood asked, puzzled because clearly no one was there but Wanda.

"I said it, young creature. My name is Voltaire, and those are my words! It is I who have spoken!"

"Voltaire, you're back!" Wanda's voice lifted with joy.

"Of course I'm back. Where else would I be?"

"Where is that voice coming from?" The Grood spun in a circle, searching for the other person who was speaking.

"Up there. In the tree." Wanda pointed to a branch overhead.

"A bird? A talking bird?" The Grood was amazed but quickly overcame her surprise. "I don't care if you're a bird who can talk. I don't care what you're saying. I want a reward." The Grood walked toward Wanda, opening and closing the very sharp scissors.

"Oh, I wouldn't do that. Don't you know, opening scissors without cutting is very bad luck," Wanda said, which was exactly the wrong thing to say.

"Bad luck for you!" said the Grood, and she lunged for Wanda. "And bad luck for your hair!"

Wanda ducked and dodged. She twisted and turned. The scissors missed Wanda's head by a mile. But they caught her nonetheless, and slit her back pocket. And out fell the one thing Wanda had managed to keep safe from the Groods—her diary.

"A book!" The Grood snatched it up and flipped through the pages. "I'll rip it to shreds. Then I'll chew on the paper. That will be fun. My very own book to devour."

"No!" Wanda couldn't bear losing her diary that way.

"Little Grood, why don't you *read* the diary instead?" Voltaire came to Wanda's rescue. "Diaries are filled with all sorts of secrets. Things I'm sure Wanda wouldn't want anyone to know. Juicy tidbits, I daresay, and more. Snooping in someone's diary is always such fun."

"Yes! Wanda's secrets!" The Grood opened the book,

and then she remembered—"I can't read," she said with immense disappointment. "I have no choice. I will have to eat it." She lifted the book to her mouth.

"No! No!" Wanda grabbed the book away from the Grood. "I'll read it to you! Let's sit."

The Grood plopped right down in front of a tree, eager to hear Wanda's most private thoughts. Even

Voltaire was curious about what Wanda had written. So the three leaned against the tree's extremely wide trunk and Wanda began to read.

"'I was born in the late afternoon, on a partly sunny day, not too hot, not too cold, on the fifth day of the fifth month, twenty-three minutes past four. I wasn't a small baby nor a big one. An average-size baby, I would say, if that's a thing that can be said about a baby. . . .'"

Wanda read and read and read. The Grood listened. Voltaire listened.

And the woods grew silent. So silent that after a while Wanda gazed up from the page—and saw that Kitten's mouth hung open and a strand of drool dribbled down her chin. Her eyes were shut tight. It appeared that Wanda's life was so dull, it had knocked the Grood out cold. Every creature nearby had also fallen fast asleep.

***

"Fascinating diary," Voltaire said politely. They were both a safe distance away now from the sleeping Grood.

"Then why are you still yawning?" Wanda frowned.

"Cheer up, dear girl. A book is a magical thing—and this one has proven it. It saved your life."

Wanda couldn't argue with that.

"And yet," he went on, "one should always aim at being interesting rather than exact."

Normally, that would have riled Wanda, but this time she replied with a simple "Uh-huh."

Voltaire flew in circles around her. "Wanda, your mind has drifted to a disagreeable place. You should order it to return at once!"

"Voltaire," she said sadly, "we've taken many different paths, and we are no closer to the cave. That's what I have been thinking. We're no closer to finding my brother. We're no closer to learning the secret of my life."

"Yes, but—"

"My brother is trapped, and he needs *me* to find him." Wanda looked up to the sky, as if the stars could show her the way. "I cannot fail him—but that is exactly what I am doing. I am failing him, and I am failing myself."

"But, Wanda—"

"No, Voltaire. There are no 'buts.' I have faded to smoke, nearly been drowned, and turned into a squid—"

"Yes, however—"

"—torn limb from limb practically twice, and came close to exploding—"

"Yes, Wan— Exploding? Really? I seem to have missed that."

"Oh, it was terrifying. It happened right after you flew off," Wanda said. "Voltaire! I almost forgot! I need to apologize. I think I insulted you. All these things that happened—none of them were your fault. But I said they were, and so I don't blame you for leaving me. Not one bit . . ."

Voltaire, who had been fluttering above Wanda's head, lowered himself for an eye-to-eye talk. "Wanda, there is no need to apologize. You did not insult me. I merely flew off in search of a safe path to take. The right path to take. I was trying to protect you from further harm. And I have succeeded. I have found it. I have found the right path. And that is what I have been trying to tell you."

"The right path! That's excellent news!" Wanda's eyes gleamed with new hope. "Which is the right path?"

"The one that will take us to the cave, of course."

Oh, nooo. Wanda moaned. *Another dead end.*

Voltaire rose in the air. He flew a few yards ahead, to a path edged in little white flowers. "And here it is!"

"Really?" Wanda asked, feeling hopeful again. She practically skipped to the trail. It was an uphill path that wound its way in and out of the trees.

"While I was searching the woods, I suddenly realized

that these bunchberry flowers will direct us to the top of the mountain—exactly where we need to go!"

"What good luck that this came to you!" Wanda said.

"Yes, I believe I always knew it, of course. But it slipped from my mind, as these things can. And then it slipped right back in again—like magic, I'd say."

So, under the glow of the moon and the light of the stars, the two followed the path of the bunchberries. They were hungry and tired, but now that they knew the right path to take, Wanda thought that nothing could stop them. . . .

Until something did.

TWENTY-TWO

What Took You So Long?

The bunchberry path was steep and difficult to climb, but Wanda was strong and determined. A promise made was a promise kept, and Wanda had promised herself that she would not fail her brother or herself. So she climbed and climbed and climbed.

The air turned chillier the higher they went. The flowers thinned out and soon disappeared. The moon drifted behind the clouds and abandoned them, too.

Wanda shivered. She hadn't eaten all day, and her empty stomach churned with hunger. But even though she was famished and cold, her good mood could not be snuffed out.

"I have a wonderful feeling about this new path," she told Voltaire. "We will find the cave. I know it now more than ever. And nothing can stand in our way."

And that's when they came to an unexpected halt. As they rounded a curve, an old shack rose up on the path, and the path ended right at its door.

The shack was tucked into a stand of trees. It was made from the same wood and blended in so well that it nearly faded from sight.

Its walls were splintered and rotted, with places gouged by the blows of an ax. In the front were the remains of a covered porch—a wooden rail hanging, floorboards crumbling.

Wanda gazed up at the shack's rusted tin roof. It sagged in the middle, and a crooked chimney poked through one side.

The front of the shack had no windows, only a door with jagged scars etched in its wood. One couldn't help but imagine that a horrible thing might be hidden inside.

If a house can look evil, this one certainly does, Wanda was thinking, when Voltaire's voice broke through.

"A shack. How delightful! Let's go inside."

"Voltaire, I don't think so." Wanda pointed to the chimney and its dirty gray smoke billowing into the sky.

"Someone is in there." She hugged herself to ward off the chill that ran through her.

"Even better," he said. "We're tired and hungry. It's a good place to rest. And if someone *is* there, they'll have food to share."

"No, I don't like the looks of it," Wanda said. "Let's go around it and be on our way."

But the bird ignored her and flew to the door. He peered into a gap between two planks. "There's lovely candlelight inside, and a stove, and a pot that is pleasantly steaming." He tried to convince Wanda to stay. "You must eat and rest. Please, knock on the door."

Wanda tried to hold back, but suddenly she couldn't resist a warm place to sit and hot food to eat. It had been days since she'd had a cooked meal.

She stepped slowly onto the rickety porch. The wood creaked under her weight, so she waited a moment to make sure it would hold her. She stared at the door. It hung askew on its hinges, and the doorknob, once bronze, had turned flaky and green.

She raised her hand and knocked twice.

"Hello?" she called out.

No one answered.

"Oh, well, we'll have to go," she said, relieved that no one had replied.

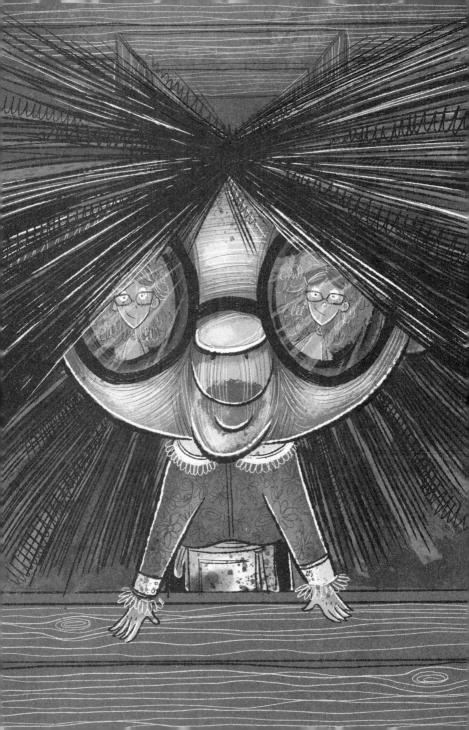

"Hold on. Just give it a minute." Voltaire hopped on her shoulder, but Wanda turned to leave. And just as she did, the door slowly scraped open.

In the flickering light stood a hunched old woman. Her face was a perfect oval with high, full cheekbones. Her dry black hair looked lifeless and scratchy and hung on each side of her head like the whisks of a broom.

Her skin was brown and wrinkled. Wanda's glance moved from the bright pink lipstick smeared on her lips to her big eyeglasses and large round eyes, blacker than night.

She was wearing a bright flowered shirt and orange pants with an apron tied around her waist. A crisp white apron splattered with ugly red stains.

"Come in, Wanda," she said. Her black eyes narrowed. "What took you so long? You're late."

100% Accurate 30% of the Time

"How do you know my name?" Wanda asked, speaking loudly to mask the tremble in her voice. "How did you know we were coming?"

"I know everything. I am the All-Knowing Phyllis," the woman said, and yanked Wanda inside. Voltaire flew in behind her and landed on a small square table in the center of the room.

"The All-Knowing Phyllis?" Wanda rubbed her arm where the woman had gripped it.

"Yes, I am the All-Knowing Phyllis."

"So nice to meet you," Voltaire said. "Do you really know everything?"

"Yes, I do," the woman confirmed.

"Then let's begin right away. There's so much I've forgotten. Please tell me all of it."

"Not *that* kind of everything." The woman shook her head. "I just know the future." Then she pushed Wanda toward one of the two chairs at the table.

"Have a seat." She slammed the shack door. "You never know who you'll meet in the Scary Wood. Can't be too careful." She slid two bolts across the door, then, for good measure, locked it with a key.

While Wanda sat, the woman tucked the key deep inside her apron pocket, which made Wanda very uncomfortable. She tried to hide her distress by gazing around the room. A shabby couch stood against one wall. An old refrigerator, stove, and sink lined another. Stubs of flickering candles sat on a small table in front of an armchair. A crackling fire warmed the shack.

"Why do you live in the Scary Wood?" Wanda asked. "If you're worried about what's out there, I mean."

"I like the quiet," Phyllis said. "It's peaceful here—except for the occasional scream."

Was that a joke? Wanda wondered. She didn't think so—Phyllis wasn't smiling. "Well, if you know everything, what can you tell us?" Wanda asked, trying to hide her fear.

Phyllis took a seat facing Wanda and the bird. "I can

see what is to be seen. I can tell what is to be told," she said. "Usually."

"Yes. Right. You're a fortune-teller," Wanda said. "Where's your crystal ball?"

"I don't use a crystal ball. I look into your eyes. Then you look into my eyes. That sort of thing."

"And that works?" Wanda's fear of the woman started to fade. *She doesn't seem dangerous at all,* Wanda thought. *More likely, she's crazy.*

"You don't believe me?" Phyllis said. "I bet you think I'm crazy." She leaned forward and stared deeply at Wanda—and Wanda could see that the woman's black eyes were like mirrors. She saw herself reflected in each of them.

"So thrilling!" Voltaire said. "Wanda, don't blink. She's going to tell you your future."

Phyllis stared hard into Wanda's eyes.

Wanda stared back.

"Yes, yes, look into my eyes . . ." Phyllis said, "and I will learn what there is to be learned. I am one hundred percent accurate thirty percent of the time."

"But that means you—" Wanda started.

"Shush!" Phyllis narrowed her eyes. "Yes, there it is. You are headed for danger."

"What kind of danger?" Voltaire flapped his wings. "What do you see? What do you see?"

"I see . . . a cave," she declared. "You are searching for a cave."

"Outstanding!" Voltaire chirped. "So true!"

"Your destiny is to reach the cave."

That prediction made Wanda very happy. Although her confidence in the bird might have wavered at times, her faith in him had remained intact. But still, it was comforting to hear news of the cave from someone else. Comforting and encouraging. And now she was convinced that this strange woman did, indeed, have some sort of power.

"And I see a boy in the cave."

"Voltaire, you were right! He *is* in the cave!"

The bluebird puffed out his chest, so proud.

"And I see dragons. They live near the cave."

"Dragons? No, you don't see dragons." Voltaire shook his head. "Please don't see dragons."

"The All-Knowing Phyllis is never mistaken. Generally. Typically. Well, not often. Anyway, I see dragons."

"What do we do about these dragons?" Wanda asked, trying to stay calm.

"Depends," said Phyllis.

"Depends on what?" Wanda asked.

"Depends on if they're the nice dragons or the not-so-nice dragons."

"Well, which ones are they?" Wanda asked.

"You're not supposed to ask questions," said Phyllis. "Nobody asks questions. They just *ooh* and *aah*. Why are you asking so many questions?"

"Well, it's kind of important to know," Wanda said. "Which dragons are they?"

"Another question. No more questions!" The All-Knowing Phyllis's gaze was broken. She blew out an exasperated breath. "Listen, I don't like people. But you seem okay, so I'm trying to help you. *Be patient!* The information doesn't all come at once."

"Maybe we could try again tomorrow?" Wanda asked.

Phyllis stood up from her chair. "We'll see. Now, stop talking. Let's eat. I knew you'd be hungry, so I cooked."

Wanda tried to press Phyllis to go on, but the woman had already walked to the stove. She removed the lid on the pleasantly steaming pot, and the room filled with the wonderful aroma of freshly made stew.

Wanda's stomach gurgled at the smell. She was *very* hungry . . . and the stew smelled *so* delicious . . . but

Wanda worried. She didn't know a thing about this woman. She *did* know these woods, though. She had been kidnapped in them, turned to smoke, and nearly changed into a squid. Could she trust anyone who lived here? Wanda stared at her plate.

"Eat it. It won't kill you," Phyllis said. "That's one hundred percent accurate."

Wanda looked at Voltaire. Was that a flicker of fear in his eyes?

She took a deep breath—and inhaled the stew's incredible aroma. It was hypnotizing, and she couldn't resist it a moment longer.

They ate at the foot of the fire. Wanda finished every morsel and licked the fork clean. She hadn't felt this cozy in days, and soon she and Voltaire fell asleep in front of the hearth, just as the All-Knowing Phyllis knew that they would.

***

The next morning, Wanda woke up to Voltaire's happy tweets. "You're in a good mood," she said.

"It's always a fine day when you discover you haven't been poisoned," he chirped.

"Voltaire," Wanda said, shaking her head, "if you were worried about the stew, why didn't you say something last night—*before* we ate it?"

"Because, Wanda dear, it wasn't a problem *before* we ate it. It would only become a problem *after* we ate it."

I guess that makes sense, Wanda thought. *Sort of. Oh, well, it really doesn't matter now. The important thing is we're still alive!*

The fortune-teller was nowhere to be seen. While they waited for her to return, Wanda and Voltaire reviewed what they had learned the night before.

"We will reach the cave—that's a sure thing," said Wanda. "But there will be danger nearby."

They wondered which dragons they would meet. And what they would do when they met them. And, most of all, they wondered what made the not-so-nice dragons not so nice.

"Even though we know about the dragons and the danger and my destiny, I'm more puzzled now than I was before," Wanda said. "Isn't it strange that the more we learn, the less we seem to know?"

"A million questions just lead to a million more," Voltaire agreed.

Just then, Phyllis came through the door with a stack of firewood in her arms.

"Oh, good," said Wanda. "You're back. We didn't want to leave without saying good-bye."

"I know," said Phyllis.

"And I wanted to talk to you one last time."

"I knew that, too."

Wanda took a deep breath. "Please, Phyllis, could you look into my eyes again and see what can be seen?" she asked. "Who is holding my brother in the cave? Why is he there?"

"Sorry." The All-Knowing Phyllis turned her hands up and shrugged. "I've already told you all there was to tell."

"How about the dragons?" Wanda wouldn't give up. "Can you tell us what they do?"

"Aha! I did have a vision of that as I closed my eyes late last night. The not-so-nice dragons turn people to ash with one single breath."

"And the nice ones?" Wanda asked.

"They don't."

"That's it?" Wanda asked.

"Afraid so," Phyllis replied.

She stood in the open doorway as Wanda and Voltaire got ready to leave.

"It's been—" Wanda started.

"A real pleasure, I know," Phyllis said. "You were

happy to meet me, and you hope to see me again soon."
With a gentle push, she guided them out.

Phyllis's dark gaze followed Wanda and Voltaire as
they made their way down the path. "Be careful and
good luck!" she called after them. "You'll need it. . . ."

TWENTY-FOUR

A Sign

"This apple is delicious!" Wanda took another bite. "So juicy. Want a piece?" She offered it to the bird on her shoulder.

Wanda had new clothes, food, a quickly drawn map, and a new rucksack to put it all in. Phyllis had known exactly what Wanda would need and had packed the rucksack full. Wanda was very grateful.

She and Voltaire picked up the trail that wound its way around the mountain. With boulders on one side and trees on the other, it was a tricky climb. Small stones along the path caused Wanda to stumble. Large leaps were required to jump over big rocks. At times the path became so narrow, her arm scraped up against the boulders. The ride became too bumpy for Voltaire, who decided to fly instead.

But through it all, Wanda remained cheerful. After a night at the shack, she felt revived and refreshed and more than ready to continue their quest.

"A mood improves quickly when you're not hungry or tired," Voltaire said.

"Yes, it does," Wanda agreed, taking another bite of her apple.

"You know, that's the secret to getting things done." Voltaire flew just ahead of her. "Throughout life, the most important decision you make is to be in a good mood." Then he flew back to her. "Today will require a very good mood if we are to battle dragons."

Dragons.

Wanda had been thinking about dragons all morning, and the mention of them caused her stomach to flip. How could a girl and a bird defeat such fearsome creatures?

"Voltaire, you know so much about so much. Do you have any idea how to fight dragons?"

"Yes, of course," Voltaire said. "There are many ways to eliminate, obliterate, annihilate, exterminate, eradicate, or decimate a dragon."

"Well, how 'bout we start with three," Wanda said. "Tell me three ways to slay a dragon."

"Certainly," Voltaire said. "You can poke him in the eyes. Then slay him when he can't see. Or you can stab him once and quickly, directly in the heart—a very sensitive spot. But if you lack something sharp, poison will work just as well."

Hmm. Wanda set her mind to thinking. *I wonder if a dragon would be willing to trade—take someone in our place. We could give the dragon my brother Zane. A beast for a beast. That could work out very nicely.* She didn't say any of this aloud, because she had promised herself to try to be kinder, especially where Zane was concerned. Instead, she asked, "Exactly how many of those methods have you seen actually work?"

"Let's see . . ." Voltaire fell behind Wanda as he counted. "Exactly . . . none," he pronounced. "Very good, Wanda," he yelled up ahead. "You've made an excellent point. I can't say with certainty that any one of those would work."

"I suppose it *is* very good, because they all seem too cruel," she called back.

She rounded a steep curve and lost sight of Voltaire. She took a few more steps, then reached into her rucksack for Phyllis's map. The old woman had done a quick job with the drawing, but it was clear that soon after this curve, the dragons would be in sight. Wanda's heart clenched at the mere thought of seeing them.

"Well, if you cannot bring yourself to slay a dragon, then we should give up our quest," Voltaire shouted.

"Give up our quest! Voltaire, did you really say that? I will never give up my quest to find my brother—no matter what danger lies ahead."

There was no question that Wanda meant what she said, but with each step that brought her closer and closer to the dragons, she grew more and more anxious.

Which dragons will we meet? she wondered.

The nice ones, she hoped—and that's what she was thinking when she tripped and lurched into a wooden post on the path. "Voltaire, come quick," she called. "I've found a sign."

"A good sign or a bad sign?"

"It's a real sign," she answered. "Come see what it says."

Voltaire's wings flapped hard as he caught up to Wanda. He found her shaking her head, staring at the small wooden post with a top carved in the shape of an arrow. And the words:

"How very thoughtful." Voltaire headed in the direction of the arrow.

"No! Come back!" Wanda said. "I think this could be a trap."

"A trap?" Voltaire returned. "How so?"

"Isn't it strange for someone to leave a sign to a hidden cave that we happen to be searching for? No one with good intentions would leave a sign like that," Wanda reasoned. "If we go that way, a trap surely awaits us. So we should go the opposite way. . . ."

"Very good." Voltaire started to fly off in the other direction.

"Unless they want us to think we should go the opposite way—and *that's* where the trap lies. So, in that case, following the arrow would be the right thing to do."

"Just where I was going." Voltaire started again.

"Unless . . ."

Voltaire stopped. "Wanda, I will follow you to the ends of the earth—but only in one direction. You must choose a path."

Wanda paced in front of the sign, trying to decide which direction to take. She consulted Phyllis's map again, but it lacked the detail they needed.

"Voltaire, you know these woods better than I do. What do your instincts tell you? Which way should we go?"

The bird perched on top of the sign. He looked to the left, and he looked to the right. He looked up; he looked down. "Gadzooks! I know this place! We'll follow the arrow."

TWENTY-FIVE

A Hunch

Wanda worried about the path they were on. She would have worried no matter which path they had taken and no matter who had selected it. And no matter how logical the choice had seemed. She worried because she knew that the only thing you could count on in the Scary Wood was that you couldn't count on anything here.

Were they headed into a trap? Her anxiety chased all thoughts of dragons from her mind as they made their way up the mountainside.

As they neared the crest, the path became rougher, then narrower. Finally it ended at two huge boulders, skyscraper tall and just as wide.

Wanda studied the stone giants. There was just a slice of daylight between them. With Voltaire on her shoulder, she drew in her breath to make herself thinner. She pressed her arms tightly to her sides and slowly wedged her way through the tight space.

"Good work!" Voltaire cheered when they stepped free of the stone. "And look where we are!"

They had reached the very highest point of the mountain. At last.

On one side of them grew a thicket of trees. Directly in front stretched a wide-open space—a rocky plateau, ending at a dizzying cliff. Wanda moved to the edge. She looked down at the terrifying drop. She had never stood on anything this high before—and it caused her to swoon. She quickly moved away from the rim.

"Voltaire, we're here! We're finally here. My brother is so close—I can feel it!"

The bluebird fluttered happily over Wanda's head. "Yes! We have done it! The cave must be right through those trees. And look, Wanda, there's not a dragon in sight. Let's hurry!"

The two had just started off again when a powerful roar shattered the heights. It made the ground rumble, and the trees shook from their roots.

And suddenly, thundering through the grove,

stomped four startling dragons, one blue, one green, one purple, and one red. As they charged from the trees into the sunlight, their scales flared and shimmered. It made for a dazzling spectacle, both splendid and fearsome.

When the dragons reached the clearing, they all spread their wings wide. Their span was enormous. Wanda had never seen such an astounding display.

With a slow grace and at exactly the same time, the dragons lifted their wings over their heads. When they spotted Wanda, they started beating their wings with fury, all the while their feet remaining firmly planted on the ground.

Wind whipped and dust churned around Wanda. The treetops bowed low. Voltaire tumbled in the air, and the gusts pushed Wanda back, back, back toward the edge of the cliff.

"Oh, noooo!" she cried.

But just as she was about to topple over the edge, the dragons folded their wings and the wild wind stopped.

Wanda fell to her knees and swallowed great gulps of air.

"Quite impressive, Wanda, wouldn't you say?" Voltaire drifted down to the ground and stared at his own small wings.

"WHO ARE YOU? WHY ARE YOU HERE?" the blue

dragon asked in a voice that was deep and strong and exceptionally loud.

Before Wanda could answer, Voltaire stepped forward.

"No, Voltaire!" Wanda lunged after him. "They will turn you to ash in one single breath."

"Don't worry, Wanda. I have a hunch."

"A hunch?"

"Yes. A hunch," Voltaire said. "Follow me. We will have a talk with these fellows."

As the two moved closer, the dragons' nostrils flared.

"Voltaire, they don't look in the mood for a chat. Are you sure about this?"

"Of course I'm not sure. I have never had a hunch in my life. Although if this one works out, I will make a note to have more."

Wanda halted, but Voltaire nudged her forward. "Now listen closely," he whispered in her ear. "Here's what I think you should say to them. . . ."

TWENTY-SIX

Dragons

"Blue dragon, sir." Wanda slowly approached the four creatures. "Or is it madam? My name is Wanda Seasongood, and I humbly seek your help. We are humbly looking for a cave, and we humbly think you can assist us."

"Very good, Wanda. Exactly as I suggested. Now a little louder and a little closer. Just remember to be respectful," Voltaire coached. "I think that's the key here."

"Do you know where the cave is?" Wanda cupped her hands to her mouth and took two small steps toward the blue dragon. "I ask humbly," she shouted.

The dragons stared at Wanda
but did not reply.

"All right, then." Voltaire
rethought his approach.
"Perhaps the key is to be direct.
Just ask them who they are."

Wanda stepped closer. "Dragons,
are you . . . are you . . . nice?"

"ARE *WE* NICE?" The blue dragon
stomped forward and the rocky surface
beneath Wanda's feet cracked. A spark of
red lit up its eyes. It was clear that Wanda
had angered it, but she didn't know why.
"THE QUESTION, LITTLE GIRL, IS: ARE *YOU*
NICE?" Its voice boomed like thunder.

Wanda hadn't expected that reply, and she didn't know what to make of it. So she fell into a dumbfounded silence.

The red dragon stepped forward. "If you are nice, we will let you live, and we will help you. If you are not nice, we will kill you."

"Oh." Wanda took a giant step back. "Then you must be the not-so-nice dragons."

"NO. We are the nice dragons. The not-so-nice dragons would kill you whether you're nice or not," the red dragon continued.

"This is very confusing," Wanda said.

"Well then, pay attention," snapped the purple dragon. "If you are pleasant and warm and kind and good-natured . . ."

"And trusting and caring and giving," continued the green one, who seemed a little more patient, "we wouldn't think of harming you. How could anyone harm such a fine person like that? But if you're not those things, we will kill you. It's simple, really."

"SO WHICH ARE YOU . . . NICE OR NOT NICE?" The blue dragon snorted. "THINK CAREFULLY. YOUR LIVES WILL DEPEND ON IT."

"We're nice! We're definitely nice. We're all of those

things. Absolutely," Wanda said boldly, hoping the dragons did not notice her worry.

Her thoughts about her parents and brother hadn't always been nice. Did the dragons have the power to detect that? She'd sworn to be kinder, and she was very serious about it, but she couldn't erase her past. Still, a promise to do better should count. Would the dragons think so? Wanda's palms turned clammy with fear.

The dragons put their heads together to consider Wanda's claim. They spoke among themselves, at first quietly, in a very different tone from their recent roars, and Wanda couldn't hear them. Then their voices rose as their debate continued.

"Do you think she's telling the truth?" the blue dragon grumbled. "I sense she's hiding something."

"Could be." The red dragon snorted. "She looks shifty."

"Rotten to the core, I think," said the purple dragon. "And not terribly smart, by the way."

Wanda's shoulders slumped.

"The bird is a dimwit, too." The green dragon scowled at Voltaire. "Probably can't tell which way is up."

Voltaire let out a sad peep.

"That's enough!" Wanda shouted. "Turn me to ash, if that's what you want, but don't insult my friend!"

"Wanda, no!" Voltaire screeched.

"WELL, NOW YOU'VE DONE IT!" the blue dragon roared. "THAT'S WHAT WE WERE WAITING FOR." The dragons put their heads together once again.

They're probably deciding how to kill me. Wanda's body stiffened.

As her eyes scanned the trees searching for a way to escape, the blue dragon turned to her. "We have come to a determination. By defending the bird, you have passed our test. Wanda Seasongood, we *do* believe you are kind and nice and caring."

Wanda's muscles sagged with relief.

"*Of course* she is kind and nice and caring." Voltaire lifted his head high. "In fact, we're here to save Wanda's brother—that's a very kind and nice and caring thing to do."

"Ah, yes. The boy in the cave," the red dragon said.

Wanda gasped. "The boy in the cave! Do you know my brother? Have you seen him?"

"We have never seen the boy. We hear he lies deep inside the cavern. But the witch who imprisoned him visits the cave often," said the blue dragon.

"Yes, as recently as today, in fact," said the red one.

"She might be there still," said the green one. "With the young lass, Wren—the one who is always by her side.

So, if you are going to the cave, consider going later," he suggested. "You don't want to meet up with them."

"A witch?" Wanda inhaled sharply. "A witch has imprisoned my brother?" Her knees went wobbly. She sank to the ground to steady herself.

A witch. A few days ago, I was simply a girl wondering where I belonged—and now I am a girl who has to save her brother from the clutches of a witch.

"Voltaire, I've never fought a witch before. How can I know if I'm up to the challenge?" Wanda held her head in her hands.

"'We know what we are, but know not what we may be,'" Voltaire quoted Shakespeare.

"But that still doesn't tell me—am I a girl who can fight a *witch*? Am I a girl who can fight a witch and win?"

"Of course you can. Or maybe not." Voltaire scratched his head. "Do you have a different question I could try to answer?"

Wanda climbed to her feet and brushed herself off. She walked up to the dragons and stood so close to them she could feel their sweltering breath on her face. "Can you please tell me more about the witch?"

"Her name is Raymunda," the purple dragon said. "All the creatures of the Scary Wood fear her. I'm surprised you've never heard of her."

It seems I haven't heard of a lot of things, Wanda thought, but she only shrugged in reply.

"Raymunda rules over these mountains and all the witches who live here," the purple dragon went on.

"You mean there's more than one?" Wanda asked in astonishment. Who knew so much was going on in these woods so close to her home?

"There are many, many witches here. Now, please, do not interrupt me," the purple dragon groused. "It's not nice. There was a time, years ago, when Raymunda's powers began to weaken," he went on. "The other witches held a meeting in the deepest part of the darkest valley, and a new witch was selected to take her place. When Raymunda heard of it, she let out a shriek that echoed to the top of this mountain. And she refused to give up her throne."

The blue dragon spoke next, lowering its head to gaze directly into Wanda's eyes. "Raymunda has worked very hard to strengthen her magic. She has vowed never to be challenged again. We hear her power is fearsome now—and no witch will defy her."

"They say she can crush any creature with a mere crook of her finger," said the red dragon.

"I heard she can make your skin boil," the purple

dragon added. "And the things they say she can do with the blood of a pig would give you nightmares."

"Voltaire," said Wanda, "we must leave here at once. We need to find out why this witch took my brother— and we must save him. Let's get to the cave quickly— before it's too late."

"I'm afraid quickly is not possible," the green dragon said. "The way to the cave is thick with brambles. You'll have a slow, hard time of it."

"Then would you be so kind and blaze a trail for us with your fiery breath?" Wanda asked.

"No. We cannot," the blue dragon replied. "We are dragons, but we are not the kind who breathe fire. That is not a way we can help."

"Can you fly us up there swiftly instead?" Wanda asked.

"We have mighty wings, but we do not fly," the red one answered.

"You do not breathe fire and you do not fly." Wanda was baffled. "Just what kind of dragons are you, besides nice, that is? What *do* you do?"

"We are the dragons who knit," said the green dragon. "We create heartwarming scenes of hearth and home. Scenes of lovely fireplaces and cozy rooms in yarn of red, blue, green, and purple." He pointed to each dragon as he recited the colors.

Knitting dragons. Wanda shook her head. It was hard to believe. "How can you help us if that is what you do?"

"Because what we do is what you'll need," the blue dragon said. "And now it's time to take your measure." He called out to the others. "We have one small bird with a very large task. And an average-size girl with oversize courage."

And then they began to knit. . . .

Which is how it came to be that, a short while later, a girl and a bird set off through the brambles, wearing identical sweaters with matching hats—on their way to meet a witch.

TWENTY-SEVEN

Are You for Me or Against Me?

"Raymunda."

Wanda now had a name to say and a person to picture—although it was hard for her to imagine anyone so wicked.

"Raymunda. Raymunda."

She said it over and over again as they trudged through the brambles. It rolled on her tongue and left with a sting.

"Wanda, how do I look in my sweater and hat?" Voltaire asked.

Wanda knew he was trying to break the hold the name had on her. And it worked, at least for a moment. She looked at the bird and laughed. His sweater, just like hers, had a scene of a roaring fireplace in a room with two overstuffed chairs. A dog snoozed on a rug in front of the fire. A painting of an eagle hung on a wall over the chairs. It was just as the dragons had described—a cozy view of hearth and home. It was a sweater Wanda would never have seen on herself, and most definitely not on a bird. The same could be said of their hats, which were knitted in stripes of red, blue, green, and purple—with a red pom-pom on each at the top.

It was amazing that the dragons had made them—and even more amazing that they could knit things small enough for a bird. The sweater and hat fit Voltaire perfectly. And Wanda had to admit that in this mountain chill, the sweater was keeping her nice and warm.

"You look very good." Wanda smiled, then returned to her monotonous chant. "Raymunda. Raymunda. Raymunda." She sighed. "Voltaire, can you imagine such a horrible person?"

"Wanda, let's not judge her too harshly. After all, she sent me to you. I wouldn't have met you if it weren't for her."

Wanda stopped walking. Her head started to spin. *"What?!* Wait! You know her?"

"Why, yes, now that you mention it," Voltaire chirped. "And it's a real stroke of luck for us, wouldn't you say?"

"Voltaire, are you sure Raymunda sent you?"

"Oh, yes. It just came to me, clear as day." Voltaire perched on Wanda's arm. "Raymunda is the one who tied the note to my neck. She is the one who set us off on our little adventure. I feel so much better now that I've remembered it."

This news pressed all the air from Wanda's lungs. The witch had sent Voltaire to her. The witch had kidnapped her brother. Why? What did it all mean?

Wanda started to walk again, but she remained silent as she tried to puzzle it out. And then another thought began to take shape. The words formed in her mouth, but they stuck to her tongue. She forced herself to say them. "Voltaire, are you for me or against me?"

"Well, both, I think. I seem to be of two minds on this point. It's a bit of a muddle, I'd say." He ruffled his feathers. "But no need to harp on it—because here we are."

They had reached the cave.

Its mouth was as black as a starless night. Wanda peered in, but she couldn't see anything through the inky darkness.

Now it was Wanda who was of two minds. Part of her wanted to rush right in to find her brother; part cautioned her to wait—the witch might still be inside.

She took but a moment to decide and stepped toward the cave. "Let's go. My brother might be in danger. We'll stick to the shadows."

She reached into her rucksack for the small flashlight Phyllis had given her. "Hop on my shoulder," she told the bird. There was no time to ponder his loyalty now. Her brother was here and so were the answers to every important question she'd ever had. Heart pounding, she entered the cave.

TWENTY-EIGHT

The Boy in the Cave

The cave was musty, chilly, and damp.

The path inside sloped down and descended quickly. Wanda placed a hand on the cave wall to keep her balance. She carefully and quietly inched her way through the darkness. She wanted to shine her flashlight up ahead so she could see where she was going, but she didn't want to alert the witch. Instead, she aimed it at her feet, where it made a very small circle of light.

She and Voltaire followed the wall through twists and turns. It was difficult walking this way. And frightening. Soon she lost track of how far they'd traveled, and even

though she hadn't yet found her brother, she started to fret about finding their way back out again.

As they moved farther into the cave, the temperature dropped, and she shivered. "Are caves always this c-c-cold?" she whispered.

"Isn't it marvelous? I believe this is an ice cave," Voltaire chirped. "It's very unusual. These caves have ice even in summer."

Wanda didn't think it was marvelous at all. The cold started to settle into her limbs, and she stumbled, kicking some pebbles and sending them thudding.

She stopped—and held her breath.

Did the witch hear that?

No one leaped out at them. It appeared they were safe, at least for the moment.

They continued to follow the wall—then she tripped again, this time over a rock.

Her hand flew up. The flashlight's beam lit the passage in front of them—and she gasped.

She was in a large cavern with a craggy domed ceiling. Directly in front of her the cave narrowed, and she could see that the path was about to end in a small alcove.

Wanda focused her light on the alcove—and saw a solid block of ice, about the size of a coffin.

She took a few steps closer, and the air turned from cold to frigid. Now she and the bird were shaking and shivering. "This is an unnatural c-c-cold." Wanda's teeth chattered, and she could see her breath when she spoke.

"Oh, d-d-dear. I b-b-believe you are r-r-right," the bird agreed. "This is no ordinary ice c-c-cave. What g-g-great g-g-good f-f-fortune it is that we have these s-s-sweaters." But even the sweaters did not sufficiently warm them.

Wanda forced herself to walk into the alcove. The air here was even colder and bit her skin. She swept her light across the block of ice—and cried out. "Voltaire! Look! We've f-f-found my b-b-brother!"

A boy of about fifteen was encased in the frozen block. Even through the layers of ice, Wanda could see that he was very handsome. He had a chiseled jawline with a strong chin. High cheekbones and a perfect nose. And a crown of thick, lustrous black hair. Wanda imagined that if he opened his eyes, they would be the deepest blue. He was the most striking boy she had ever seen.

"V-v-very nice-looking lad," Voltaire said. "What a p-p-pity he's d-d-dead."

"We're t-t-too late!" Wanda moaned. She had known sadness before, but nothing that had tortured her heart this way. Her knees started to fold. She touched the block of ice to steady herself—and a frigid shock coursed through her fingers. It shot up her arm and pierced her chest like a dagger.

She let out a gasp. "Voltaire, I c-c-can't move my arms or my legs!" Her knees and elbows had begun to harden in place. Her skin started to stiffen. She struggled to breathe and fought to fill her lungs with air.

"Wanda, I b-b-believe this c-c-cave is under R-R-Raymunda's spell. Our b-b-blood is turning to ice. She is f-f-f-freezing us to d-d-death from inside and out."

The air grew more frigid. The walls in the cave became coated with frost. Wanda's bones and skin turned brittle. "I think I'm b-b-beginning to c-c-crack," she rasped.

And then, just as their blood was about to turn solid, their sweaters and hats began to glow. The cozy scenes on their sweaters flickered to life. The fire in the fireplaces appeared to blaze, and it cast a red glow on the cave walls.

All the yarn began to shimmer, and it lit up the cave in radiant hues of blue, red, green, and purple.

The air quickly grew warmer.

The frost on the walls began to melt.

And Wanda could feel her blood flowing through her veins again. Her arms and legs tingled with warmth.

"The dragons' sweaters are saving our lives!" She hugged herself and ran her fingers over the magical yarn.

"Voltaire, how are you feeling?" she asked, concerned about the fragile bird.

"My hat is heating my head very nicely," Voltaire observed. "I never considered wearing a hat before, but now I shall think twice about leaving home without it."

Wanda and Voltaire continued to grow warmer—and so did the air around them.

Drip. Drip. Drip.

The air had grown so warm, the coffin of ice began to melt.

The magical sweaters continued to glow. They glowed until the air in the cave was extremely toasty—and all that was left of the icy coffin was a very large puddle on the cave floor. Then they stopped.

"Look!" Wanda's gaze rested on the boy, whose eyelids had begun to flutter. "He's alive! He's alive!"

Wanda and Voltaire watched in silence as the boy moved his arms and legs, bending them, stretching them, testing them. Then he opened his eyes and caught sight of the girl and the bird.

"Hello." His voice was dry and whispery. "Hello," he tried again, and this time it came out stronger and clearer. "My name is William."

"My—my name is Wanda. I'm your long-lost sister!"

Wanda's heart filled with a joy she had never known before.

William slowly sat up. "I've been under a terrible spell," he said. "And somehow you've managed to free me. But I believe you have mistaken me for someone else."

"I'm not mistaken," Wanda said, nodding with confidence, "although I can understand your shock. I am your sister."

The boy smiled at Wanda. "I hate to disagree with you, since you've just saved my life, but I am very certain of it—I am not your brother."

TWENTY-NINE

I've Made a Slight Error

Voltaire hopped on the boy's knee. "Evidently, this young man is in some sort of stupor," he said to Wanda.

"Try to concentrate," he suggested to William. "You've been in a deep freeze, and perhaps your brain has not quite defrosted. This is Wanda. Wanda, your sister."

The boy listened to Voltaire, then turned to Wanda. "I'm sure it would be very nice to be related to you, but if you were my sister, I would know it."

"Voltaire, how can this be?" Wanda's face creased in confusion.

"Let me think." The little bird paced in front of the boy. "Yes! Something has just come to me!" He stopped and looked up at Wanda. "I've made a slight error. The boy in the cave is not your brother." He turned to William. "But aren't you somebody's brother?"

"Yes, I am." William rose to his feet and tested his legs. "I am a brother to a brother—and his name is Zane."

"ZANE?!" Wanda cried. "That's impossible. Zane is *my* brother."

"No, Wanda. Zane is *his* brother," Voltaire chirped.

"What do you mean Zane is his brother?" Wanda slumped against the cave wall. The threads of her life were suddenly unraveling, and she felt like loose, dangling strings of cloth.

"I recall it all now. Pity I couldn't remember it sooner," Voltaire said. "The witch told me everything—but I've simply mixed up the brothers. Sometimes things get a bit jumbled up here." The bird lifted his foot and scratched his head.

"I thought I had at least one brother," Wanda said, "and now I have none."

"Not to worry, Wanda," Voltaire said. "A brother was missing and a brother was found. A good day all around, don't you think?"

Wanda's thoughts were in a whirl. She took a deep breath to calm herself. "Voltaire, you said the witch told you everything. What else did she say?"

"I believe you know all of it now, dear Wanda. Oh, wait. Did I tell you about my mission?"

Wanda held her breath. She slowly shook her head no.

"The witch told me to lead you into the Scary Wood, where you'd most certainly die. It would stop you from snooping. From uncovering her secret. From ruining all her plans."

"Oh, no." Wanda gasped. Voltaire had been plotting against her this whole time. The ground beneath her began to spin.

I was right, she thought with a heavy heart. *Voltaire led me to the Groods, and the swamp goblin, and the horrible nixie.* Wanda trembled at the thought of it. She could barely look at the bird she had considered her one true friend. Her head hung down in despair.

"Is there anything else you need to tell me?" she asked.

"That's it"—he gave a satisfied nod—"except for one last thing. . . ."

She held her breath while Voltaire tried to recall the one last thing. She reached out for the wall, unsure if she could remain standing for yet another surprise.

"Aha! Now I remember. I refused to help her. I wanted no part of it. But then things became foggy—well, foggier than usual—and the next thing I knew, I was flying into your window."

"The witch must have put you under one of her spells," William told Voltaire. "They tend to make you dizzy and muddle the mind. It's the sort of thing she loves to do."

"How do you know what the witch loves to do?" Wanda asked. "Do you know her that well?"

"I know her quite well," he answered. "The witch is my mother."

THIRTY

An Exemplary Witch

Wanda sat down on the cold cave floor.

"The witch—Raymunda—is your mother?" She had heard William perfectly, but she needed to say it again and out loud for it to become real.

"Yes, yes, she is," William said, and shrugged.

How could a mother bury her son in ice? And how could a son seem to take it so calmly?

It was all so . . . *unthinkable.*

Wanda insisted that they leave the cave and find a place to sit under a tree. A place where she could catch her breath. Absorb everything she had heard. And try to find out how she fit into this mess.

William was excited to leave the cave—to see flowers and trees, the sky and the sun, the whole world again. "Is it day or night?" he asked, bounding ahead before Wanda had a chance to aim her flashlight.

"It's probably dark out by now," she said. She pointed the light in front of her—and caught sight of a shimmering object on the cave floor. She picked it up and placed it in the palm of her hand.

It looked like part of a necklace. *A locket?* she wondered. The case was made of lapis, and Wanda admired its deep blue color. *The color of the sky at midnight,* she thought. She stared at the streaks of glittering gold that ran through it. "Like little moonbeams," she whispered as the rays stretched out to her. She tucked the beautiful trinket safely in her pocket to study it later in better light.

Once out of the cave, William took deep, deep breaths, as if trying to inhale all the lost time he'd spent in his tomb. Then he sat under a tree next to Wanda with Voltaire perched on the top of Wanda's hat.

"I hope you don't think I'm rude," Wanda said to William, "but I have so many questions. And you seem to be fine, so I'll just start right in." Wanda knew she was inches away from learning the secret of her life, and she simply couldn't wait any longer. "Why did your mother put you under this horrible spell, and why does she want to destroy me? Do you know the answers?"

"Yes, I do," William replied. "But first—how much do you know about witches?"

"Not much," Wanda said. "Only what I've read in fairy tales. It wasn't until today that I learned that they're real."

"Well, the most important thing to know about witches is that they love one thing above all else, and

that is power. Anyone who stands in the way of them getting it, keeping it, or growing it stronger is doomed," he said. "And you are in my mother's way. The same is true for me and for Zane."

"Wanda, isn't this thrilling?" Voltaire flew to the ground and hopped up and down. "A witch is out to get you! Now you'll have something exciting to write in your diary." He gathered some leaves to settle into a comfy seat.

"How can I be in your mother's way?" Wanda asked, trying to focus on what William was saying. "I don't even know her."

"Actually, you do, although somewhat by accident," William said with a smile.

Though William's smile was a little sad, Wanda thought it was still very nice. She looked into his eyes and saw that they were the exact shade of blue she had imagined. There was something mesmerizing about this boy, and she suddenly wished they didn't have to spend any more time talking about witches.

"A witch's power needs to be fed," William continued. "Some witches feed on hatred. Others on greed, jealousy, fear, or lies. There's a coven for each of these traits—five covens in all—and every witch belongs to one of them."

"Which coven does your mother belong to?" Wanda thought it would be important to know.

"None of them," William replied. "Mother is what they call an *Exemplary*. She feeds on all of those things. That's why she is so powerful, and why she is the leader of the covens. Exemplaries are very rare. But you know two of them—my mother and Zane."

"Zane is a witch?" Wanda couldn't believe it at first, but then she had to admit it made sense. He was definitely evil enough. . . .

Then a piercing thought stabbed Wanda. "That means you must be a witch, too. . . ." She shifted away from William.

William shook his head. "No, I have no magical powers of any kind." He gazed down as if embarrassed, then lifted his head to look at Wanda. "Of course, one can learn to become a witch. You don't have to be born into it. But I don't seem to have the talent to learn, either." He laughed. Then his smile faded as he continued his story. "Over the course of her life, my mother has had many enemies—and one of them cast a deadly spell on her. An extraordinary spell. Day by day it weakened her powers and slowly drained her life away. Everyone knew that the time would soon come when Zane would have to take her place."

"This is all very fascinating," Voltaire said. "But what exactly does it have to do with our Wanda?"

"Exactly this," William replied. "My mother craves power and will do *anything* to hold on to it. She would never allow *anyone* to take her place, including Zane."

Wanda's toes curled inside her shoes. She didn't know where this was heading, but she knew it wasn't going to be good.

"She tried to turn Zane into an animal. But she was too weak, Zane was too strong, and the spell didn't quite work. She turned him into something half boy, half creature, and he ran away."

That certainly sounds like Zane, Wanda thought. She wondered what he was like before the spell, but she didn't want to interrupt William to ask.

"We found him in your arbor, growling and howling," William continued, "and he refused to return with us. So, with the little magic she had left, she bewitched your family. She made you all think that Zane was one of your own. She put your parents in a trance, convincing them to tend to Zane above all else. Then she silenced me in a prison of ice—a spell that you managed to break." William slouched against the tree and relaxed. "Thank you for that."

The haze over Wanda's life had finally cleared. Now everything made sense. The strange way her parents treated her. Zane's beastly behavior. The constant feeling that something wasn't quite right.

She felt a sudden lightness and knew that the witch's spell no longer clung to her. Any lingering weight of the curse had lifted. The locket in her pocket grew warm, and she took it out to gaze at it.

"What's that?" William asked, seeing the glow in her hand.

"Just something I brought from home." Wanda slipped it back in her pocket, not ready to share what she had found. "And speaking of home, I must go back and break the spell on Zane and my parents." Wanda jumped up. "How do we do that? We must do it at once!"

William lowered his head to think. "We'll have to go to the witches' garden, in the darkest part of the deepest valley. That's where the plants for the potions grow. We can gather what we need there to end the spell."

When he gazed up, his eyes gave away a new thought taking shape. But he offered nothing more—except a narrowed glance and a slow, mysterious smile.

THIRTY-ONE

The Witches' Garden

The next morning, as the dark surrendered to a brightening sky and the flicker of the last star faded, the three prepared to leave. It was important to get an early start. It would take all day to make their way down the mountain, then till evening to reach the witches' garden.

There was a chill in the air, and Wanda and Voltaire still wore their matching sweaters and hats. Now that William could see them clearly in the morning light, he couldn't help but stare. "Do you two always dress alike?" he asked.

"These sweaters saved our lives," Wanda explained. "And yours, too." She told him about their encounter with the dragons and how the sweaters had melted the ice.

"The nice dragons—of course. I should have recognized their knitting." He touched the yarn on Wanda's sleeve. "There's nothing like dragon yarn. Legend says it has many ways of protecting someone from harm."

Voltaire stuck out both wings. "And the colors really look splendid against my blue feathers, don't you think?"

As they traveled down the mountain, the air grew warmer. Wanda and Voltaire removed their sweaters and hats, and Wanda made sure to tuck them safely in her rucksack.

They followed a winding path until it split in two. William had been guiding them, but he hesitated at the fork.

"I must admit," he said. "I'm not entirely sure which path to take. My memory seems a little foggy." He squinted and gazed down each trail. "I guess my mind hasn't cleared yet from my mother's deep chill."

"Your mother is a horrible, terrible, despicable person," Wanda said. "She confused Voltaire the same way, and because of her, I was nearly killed three times before I found you."

William frowned but didn't say anything.

"I'm feeling much more myself now," Voltaire said,

fluttering above them. "I think I can deduce the way from here. We will take the path on the right. Then we'll look for the moss on the trees—it grows only on the north side. Eventually we will turn left at the dwarf pitch pines and head south. And then we'll be there. It's simple, really."

"How do you know all this?" William asked.

"Voltaire is very smart. When he isn't all mixed up, that is." Wanda smiled and started along the path the bluebird had suggested.

"Thank you, Wanda," said Voltaire. "Nice of you to notice."

They continued in silence, each deep in their private thoughts. Wanda's drifted between Zane and her parents.

"You don't have to worry—your brother is fine." Even though William hadn't asked about Zane, she thought he would want to know. "He hasn't been easy to live with, though," she let slip. "He has the manners of a beast."

"Understandable," said William, "since Mother turned him into one, at least partially." His face lit up with a grin.

"Oh, sorry. That's right," Wanda apologized. "It will be wonderful to break the spell he and my parents are under and have them back the way they should be. I wonder what the real Zane will be like."

"Well, before the spell, he was very charming. Even as a baby he could make anyone give him whatever he wanted." William grinned. "But that was okay, since he shared everything with me."

"Being so close—it must have been nice," Wanda said.

"Yes, it was," William agreed. "We were brothers, and we were best friends."

"I wish I had a brother or sister to go home to," Wanda said.

Wanda wasn't certain William had heard her. A shadow passed over his face and his smile faded. "My mother always said that Zane had incredible power from the day he was born. Now that he's older, I'm sure his powers have grown even stronger. Having that much power can be dangerous." William shook his head and grew quiet. All talk of Zane ended there.

As night approached and they neared the darkest part of the deepest valley, the topic returned to covens and witches.

"Every time someone lies or is greedy or jealous, a witch is encouraged," William explained. "Anytime someone acts with hatred or causes fear, a witch grows stronger. Evil feeds evil, and there seems to be no end to it. It's all very good for the witches." He shrugged.

"Yes, dear boy," Voltaire said. "But evil only wins if we

choose to do nothing about it. And we're doing our part, aren't we?" Voltaire's eyes narrowed with determination. "Look—I believe we're here!"

Just ahead of them Wanda saw an old stone house with a flight of stone steps leading up to it. The house was completely surrounded by tall trees, and Wanda had to peer between the tree trunks to get a glimpse of it. The light of the moon made it easy enough to see.

The house stood two stories high. It was made of gray stone, but most of it was covered with a thick green blanket of moss. The slate roof came to a point, and just beneath the roof's peak, a small, round window was set into the front of the house. Although the other windows in the house were dark, a soft yellow glow filled this one.

"I think someone's inside," Wanda whispered.

"Probably so," William said. "The witches come here to meet and practice their spells. It's a safe place for them."

They walked closer, with Voltaire flying just ahead of them, and Wanda could see that the house was larger than a first glance revealed. It extended far back into the woods. There was another stone staircase at the back. "Those steps will take us down to the garden," William said, and headed toward them. "Let's try to be quiet.

Witches have excellent hearing, and it would be best not to disturb them."

They stepped very carefully, trying to avoid anything on the ground that might snap or crunch. When they reached the bottom of the stairs, Wanda saw a huge plot of land with trees far in the distance. But there was not a single plant in sight. The land was bare.

"Where is the garden?" she whispered.

"It's right here." William took Wanda by the shoulders and positioned her directly in front of him, facing out. "Now you should be able to see it." Voltaire settled on the top of her head.

As Wanda stared at the vacant earth, shafts of moonlight twisted and bent until they were shining directly on the empty field. Then the air began to shimmer— and plants sprouted from the ground, taking shape as if summoned into being.

Wanda gasped. "Did *you* do that?" She turned to William. "I thought you said you weren't a witch."

William shook his head. "It's the magic of the garden."

Within minutes, the garden was lush with colorful and fragrant flowers. Bright reds and pinks. Iridescent blues, yellows, and greens. Glimmering purples. And black flowers, too. They sprouted around oddly shaped

trees and bushes with bright orange berries. William told her that the flowers she thought looked the prettiest and smelled the sweetest were the most poisonous.

Stone walkways appeared, winding through the trees and flowers. And trellises with snaking vines. Common herbs grew next to strange plants Wanda had never seen before.

In the very center of the garden, there was a large circular mosaic embedded in the earth. Arranged around it were elaborately carved benches where one could sit and view the garden.

Wanda focused on the mosaic. Glittery gold and silver tiles had been set into it to form a crescent moon surrounded by twinkling stars. And Wanda saw that all the winding walkways throughout the garden eventually led to the moon.

As they walked through the shrubbery, William identified the plants they would need to undo his mother's spell.

Wanda's rucksack quickly filled with the leaves and berries they would use to make the potion. She and Voltaire sat down under a tree to arrange them all in her bag and to make room for more.

"Ah. Here's what I was looking for," William said from somewhere nearby. "The stinging nettle."

"Be careful," a silky voice warned, floating over the breeze. "Those can burn at the touch."

Wanda peered out from behind the tree. A tall, thin woman stood at the top of the stone stairs. She wore black pants, a shiny black blouse, and a long black cape that flowed to her knees. Her skin was creamy, and her jet-black hair hung in waves to her waist. Wanda's stomach twisted in fear. Was this one of the witches from the house?

"I didn't expect to see you here," the woman said.

"Is that so?" William replied without emotion. He didn't seem concerned as he stepped toward the tree where Wanda was hidden.

He's trying to block me from view, Wanda realized and moved farther back into the shadow of the tree.

But William didn't stand in front of her. Instead, he reached for Wanda's arm. He pulled her from the shadows and yanked her into a patch of moonlight. "And I bet you didn't expect to see *her,* either, Mother."

THIRTY-TWO

Never Trust a Witch

Mother?! This was Raymunda! Wanda swayed in shock. She nearly fell over, but William held her arm firmly. Voltaire fluttered up into a tree.

"Wanda. How lovely." Raymunda folded her arms tightly in front of her. She was a daunting figure—straight-backed and regal. "I don't know how you escaped the cave. I assume the nice dragons had a hand in breaking my spell. But, I must admit, I'm not totally disappointed. Thank you, William. This is a very thoughtful gift." She sauntered down one of the walkways. "It will be much more satisfying to see Wanda suffer here, where I can watch her closely."

Wanda yanked free of William. "How could you do this to me? I thought we were friends. I saved you! I trusted you!"

"William cannot be trusted." Raymunda meandered toward the center of the garden. "You have learned an important lesson, Wanda, but you've learned it too late—never trust a witch."

Wanda turned to William. "You *are* a witch? But you said . . ." She had foolishly believed him, and he had betrayed her—and she didn't know which one felt worse.

"Sorry, Wanda." His mouth twisted into a grin. "I belong to the Coven of Lies. I feed off deceit. Even my own. With every lie I told you, I felt stronger and stronger. Thanks for your help."

"You're a scoundrel!" Voltaire's wings beat hard as he flew circles around William. "Wanda, I suggest that you end your friendship with this boy at once and cut all ties to him."

"I don't think that will be a problem." Raymunda laughed. "Wanda is about to cut all ties with everyone she knows."

Wanda's heart pounded faster than Voltaire's beating wings. Everything had turned sour so quickly. But she would not allow these witches to witness her fear. "You don't frighten me," she said to Raymunda.

"Oh, but I will," the witch replied. "I will soon terrify you. And there will be no one here to help you this time. No little Grood. No nice dragons." She turned to her son. "Now, William—if you want to remain free, you must promise to leave Zane where he is. Otherwise, I will be forced to do something worse than imprison you in ice."

"That won't be necessary, Mother." William smiled. "I see that your health and powers have returned—and I would very much like to learn and work by your side."

"Good," said Raymunda. "The Five Covens have accepted my reign. They fear a war is coming with the witches from the South, and they need me to lead them. My place is secure here—unless Zane is freed. I understand that boy well. He is so much like me. He would kill me in an instant to take my place."

"I have no desire to help him or to hurt you," William said. He took Wanda's arm again. "Now, what should we do with this one?"

"Tie her up and set her at my feet." Raymunda took a seat on one of the garden benches.

"And the bird?" William asked. Voltaire had settled on Wanda's shoulder, which gave her a little comfort.

"He is no danger to us. I'll see to him later." She reached into the folds of her cape and took out her wand. "Now I will gather the other witches. I want them to witness

179

how I deal with my enemies." She waved her wand and muttered some words that Wanda guessed were a summoning spell.

William pulled out a wand he had hidden in his jacket. With a simple flick of it, a rope appeared around Wanda's wrists. As William tested the knot, Voltaire pressed up against Wanda's ear. "I will fly without rest to bring back help," he whispered. "And if you fall into despair, just remember the words of F. Scott Fitzgerald. 'You mustn't confuse a single failure with a final defeat.' See? I've said it, and I feel better already!"

And with that he flew off.

"You're right about Voltaire," William said as he tightened the knot around Wanda's wrists. "He is a smart bird. You'll never see him again."

Wanda didn't bother responding. This lying boy, raised by such a cruel and evil mother, knew nothing about the true nature of friendship.

Then, as William marched her to sit at the feet of the horrible witch, she forced all fearful thoughts from her mind to concentrate on one thing only—her plan to escape.

THIRTY-THREE

Wanda's Brew

A thousand and two witches.

The Five Covens came for Raymunda's show. Men and women of every age, race, shape, and size. They walked in through the woods, fell from the sky, or just materialized in the air with a *pop!* One old witch with a long beard arrived on a bicycle, pedaling furiously, apologizing for his lateness. Their arrival was at once spectacular and frightening.

But for Wanda, the most terrifying part was how they looked. They appeared to be everyday people—a store-keeper, a neighbor—there was nothing that set them apart from the people Wanda saw daily. *There are witches among us, and it's impossible to tell who they are.* Wanda shivered and hoped that William, standing right behind her, hadn't noticed.

The witches gathered around the circle mosaic and spilled onto the winding paths. They stood on the steps that led to the garden and on the leafy ground at the sides of the house. They surrounded Wanda, and she could not see a way to flee from them.

When the last witch, a young girl named Wren, joined them, Raymunda rose from her seat. She stepped into the middle of the circle. "Welcome, my friends. This is Wanda. Her meddling has landed her here, where no mortal should ever be. I have invited you to enjoy her punishment."

The other witches murmured their approval.

Raymunda turned to Wanda. "I thought about all the wonderful ways I could hurt you. I could make your bones twist until they crack."

"Ooh," the crowd said.

"Or have all your blood drain out through your ears."

"Aah," said the onlookers.

"I even considered having pieces of you simply fall off—your nose, a foot, a finger, an arm, every part of you dropping away, one by one."

"Ouch," said a few of the witches, clutching their noses or ears.

"But in all of these choices, you would die very quickly," said Raymunda, "and where's the fun in that?"

The witches nodded in agreement.

"No. None of those would do." Raymunda stepped toward Wanda. "I have a much better solution—a potion. Concocted especially for someone who asks too many questions."

Wanda's head buzzed with fear. She looked to the sky. Where was Voltaire? Had he found help? She wished he would hurry.

With a wave of her wand, a tarnished and dented goblet appeared in Raymunda's palm. Whatever was inside it was giving off smoke. "I call this Wanda's Brew. After just one cup of it, you will never ask another question. When you speak, it will sound like gibberish. When you write, it will come out in scribbles. *Poor Wanda*, people will say. *Her mind has turned to slush.*"

Wanda had to admit that she couldn't think of a more frightening punishment for herself, someone who had a lot to say . . . someone who wanted to be taken seriously . . . someone who needed to set things right.

Raymunda thrust the cup between Wanda's bound hands. "Drink it."

Wanda searched the sky one last time.

No Voltaire.

She looked out at the witches, who returned her gaze with cold, vacant stares.

She glanced behind her at William, who simply nodded.

She thought about her parents, and even Zane. Who would save them now?

No one. Wanda had failed them, and herself.

She had no choice.

She took the cup and drank.

THIRTY-FOUR

Give It Back!

The liquid was bitter and harsh.

Wanda spit it out.

"Drink it!" the witch commanded. "Drink it all."

Wanda's heart pounded in terror as the sour potion slid down her throat. *I will not let this drink turn my mind to slush. I will not. I will not. I will not.* She repeated this over and over again, certain that her determination would defeat the poison.

The goblet slipped from her hands as the last stinging drop rolled down her tongue.

Raymunda watched as Wanda swallowed the final bit of brew. She let out a sigh. The muscles in her face began to relax.

She waited for the potion to attack Wanda's brain. Then she allowed herself the smile she had earned.

"Who are you?" Raymunda asked. Wanda could see that she was ready to savor the gibberish she would hear.

"I am Wanda."

Gasps echoed from the crowd of witches.

"*What?!*" Raymunda's anger flared. "How can this be?" She asked again, "Who are you? Why are you here?"

"I am Wanda Seasongood. I am here to make a potion that will free my parents from your terrible spell."

The observers looked at each other in shock.

"This isn't possible!" Raymunda's body turned rigid with fury. She stared out at the witches. "Who is responsible for this?" she demanded. "Show yourself and claim this deed."

No one came forth.

The witches stared at Wanda, bewildered. Was this girl a witch? Did she have powers greater than Raymunda's?

Raymunda whirled around in confusion.

Then her eyes narrowed with horror.

Her hands flew to her throat, frantically searching her neck. "Where is it?" she howled at Wanda. "Give it back!"

"I don't have anything that belongs to you," Wanda replied.

"Do. Not. Lie. To. Me." Raymunda's jaw tightened in anger. She raised her wand in the air. "Where is it?"

"I have no idea what you're talking about," Wanda said, and it was clear to all who heard her that she was speaking the truth.

"She wants the Enlightener. The locket in your pocket," William whispered. "Don't give it to her. It has great power. It will protect you from her spells."

Why was he telling her this? she wondered. And could she believe this liar, this witch?

But something *had* protected her from Raymunda's brew.... Had William been trying to fool his mother all this time? Wanda didn't know what to think.

"Give it back NOW!" Raymunda shrieked.

"I am here!" Wanda heard the call from above, and she thought it was the sweetest sound she'd ever heard. Voltaire had returned! "And I have brought help!" The bird landed at her feet.

"Yes!" Wanda cheered. With help she was certain that she could find a way through this dark horde. But she let out a moan when she saw who Voltaire had found to rescue her.

"Hello, Princess." The frog hopped out of the crowd and onto her knee. "I heard you were in trouble. Kiss me."

THIRTY-FIVE

Blast Him

"Oh, nooo!" Wanda let out a long, loud groan.

"Kiss me, Princess. Give me another chance. Kiss me and we'll hop out of here together. It's you and me forever. Kiss me. Kiss me." The frog scrunched up his lips for a smooch.

"Voltaire, how can this frog help us?"

"He saved your life once. Perhaps he can do it again!" Voltaire chirped.

Raymunda stopped shrieking when she caught sight of the frog. She shifted her anger to the slimy pest. "William, get him!" she ordered.

William leaned over and grabbed the frog, but the wet creature slid easily from his grasp.

Wanda gazed out at all the witches gathered before her. "Voltaire, I would need a thousand and two frogs to do any good here." She shook her head, watching William at her feet, trying to pounce on the frog that kept hopping away.

"Use your wand and blast him!" Raymunda ordered her son.

"No!" Wanda cried. "Don't hurt him!"

William raised his wand.

And that's when the idea came to her. "William, if you truly want to help me, please turn this frog into a thousand and one more."

William took aim at the frog.

Wanda held her breath.

The wand came down . . .

And Wanda gasped as a hot green spark flew from it.

Kiss Me

Kiss Me

Kiss me. Kiss me. Kiss me. **Kiss me.**
KISS ME. KISS ME. Kiss me. Kiss me.
Kiss me. KISS ME. KISS ME. KISS ME.
Kiss me. **Kiss Me.** Kiss me. KISS ME. Kiss me. Kiss
me. Kiss me. Kiss me. Kiss me. Kiss me. Kiss me. Kiss
me. KISS ME. **KISS ME.** Kiss me. Kiss me. Kiss me. KISS
ME. KISS ME. KISS ME. Kiss me. KISS ME. Kiss me.
KISS ME. Kiss me. Kiss me. Kiss me. Kiss me. KISS ME.
KISS ME. **Kiss Me**
   KISS ME. Kiss me. Kiss me. Kiss me. KISS ME. KISS
ME. KISS ME. Kiss me. KISS ME. Kiss me. KISS ME.
Kiss me. Kiss me. Kiss me. Kiss me. KISS ME. KISS ME.

Kiss me. Kiss me. Kiss me. KISS ME. KISS ME. KISS ME. Kiss me. KISS ME. Kiss me. Kiss me.

Kiss me. Kiss me. Kiss me. Kiss me. KISS ME. KISS ME. Kiss me. Kiss me. Kiss me. KISS ME. **KISS ME.** KISS ME. Kiss me. KISS ME. Kiss me. KISS ME. Kiss me. Kiss me. Kiss me. Kiss me. Kiss me. Kiss me. Kiss me. KISS ME. KISS ME. Kiss me. Kiss me. KISS ME. KISS ME. KISS ME. Kiss me. KISS ME. Kiss me. KISS ME. Kiss me. Kiss me. Kiss me. Kiss me. KISS ME. KISS ME.

KISS ME. Kiss me. **Kiss me.** Kiss me. KISS ME. KISS ME. KISS ME. Kiss me. KISS ME. Kiss me. KISS ME. Kiss me. Kiss me. Kiss me. Kiss me. KISS ME. **KISS ME.** Kiss me. Kiss me. Kiss me. KISS ME. KISS ME. KISS ME. Kiss me. **KISS ME.** Kiss me.

The garden reverberated with the croaking of 1,002 frogs. They hopped on the witches. Hurled at them. Dove at them. One thousand and two frogs with lips puckering up.

The witches tripped over them. Slipped over them. They darted and dodged them. Swat, smacked, and whacked them. But that only encouraged the frogs to hop higher and faster.

KISS ME. Kiss me. KISS ME. Kiss me. KISS ME. KISS ME. Kiss me. KISS ME. Kiss me. KISS ME.

KISS ME. Kiss me. KISS ME. Kiss me. KISS ME. Kiss me. **Kiss me.** Kiss me. KISS ME. Kiss me.

KISS ME. Kiss me. KISS ME. Kiss me. KISS ME. KISS ME. Kiss me. KISS ME. Kiss me. **KISS ME.**

KISS ME. Kiss me. KISS ME. Kiss me. KISS ME. Kiss me. Kiss me. Kiss me. KISS ME.

The garden was awhirl with hopping frogs and leaping witches, and Wanda lost sight of Raymunda in the frenzy.

"Run!" William said—and the ropes that tied Wanda magically fell to the ground. "Tell Zane to meet me at the cave. Now go!"

Wanda grabbed her rucksack and ran. She raced up the garden stairs. Hurdled over witches and frogs. Dashed by the front of the house. At the edge of the trees, she took one last look back. The young girl Wren stood at the top of the garden stairs and watched her flee. Wanda felt the power of her gaze follow her as she escaped into the woods.

SS ME. Kiss me. KISS ME. Kiss me. KISS ME. Kiss me. Kiss me. KISS ME. Kiss me. KISS ME. Kiss me. KISS ME. Kiss me. Kiss me. KISS ME. Kiss

THIRTY-SEVEN

Run Faster

As the night faded and darkness lifted, it became easier to run through the woods. For a time Wanda could still hear the chattering frogs, but soon she was left with only the sounds of her pounding footsteps and her thudding heart.

She leaped over rocks and crashed through the bushes. She raced easily when there were paths to follow and struggled when there were none. But she never stopped, and she ran with only one thought in mind, and that was to run faster.

Wanda was sorry she'd had to leave Voltaire behind, but he could fly to safety and she couldn't. She hadn't had a chance to thank the royal Prince Frog, either. She was so grateful she could have . . . kissed him.

She finally slowed when she saw a flicker of light through the trees. She had reached the edge of the Scary Wood. Wanda hoped it was a magical boundary Raymunda and the other witches couldn't cross. Just beyond the tree line was an open meadow. The morning sun was on the rise. It lit up the goldenrod, and the air shimmered with a yellow glow. For Wanda it was a most beautiful sight. She stepped into the golden light and finally sat down to rest.

In her rucksack, she held everything she needed to brew a tea that would end the witch's curse. Zane would no longer be part beast, and he would return to where he belonged. Her parents would once again become the calm, caring people she had dreamed they would be. They would be proud of her for breaking the spell. And they would love her.

There would be no more great puzzle in her life, she thought—except, perhaps, for William.

Had he offered her up to his mother knowing the Enlightener would save her? Had he freed her just so she could cure Zane? What was the truth behind all his lies?

Well, it really doesn't matter, Wanda thought. *I'll never see him again.* And that brought her to the real reason she was still sitting at the edge of the Scary Wood instead of hurrying home.

Where was Voltaire? Would she ever see *him* again?

She peered into the forest, hoping he would come fluttering out. *Wanda! Wanda!* She imagined him calling her name. But she waited and waited, and he didn't appear. At first she feared he had fallen prey to the witches, but that worry quickly slipped away—Voltaire was quite capable of taking care of himself.

No, his mission is over, and he is on to something new, Wanda thought, *if he can keep in mind what the new thing is.* She smiled. Then she stood up and headed home, triumphant and sad, wondering how her heart could feel both heavy and light at the same time.

THIRTY-EIGHT

The True Zane

"I'm home!" Wanda opened the peeling and cracked yellow door to her house. She had been away for just a few days, but so much had happened to her since then. So much had changed.

Her parents rushed to the door to meet her.

"Wanda!" Her father looked puzzled. "What are you doing here?"

"You've returned too soon!" her mother shouted.

Zane bullied his way between the two and charged right into Wanda. She reeled to the left, swung an arm out for balance, and knocked over a delicate vase. It clattered to the floor with a great crash. Zane gazed down at the scattered shards, then peered up at Wanda and grinned.

"Your grandmother's vase." Her mother sighed.

"You're so clumsy." Her father shook his head in despair.

Wanda took a deep breath. She held her rucksack in front of her and gripped it tighter, protecting the plants she needed to break the spell. *William was supposed to help with this part,* she thought. *I don't know the first thing about potions.* But if she was worried, her pleasant smile didn't betray her. "Let's go into the kitchen," she said, "and I'll make some tea."

***

Wanda's mother set down her teacup and leaned back in her chair. "That tasted heavenly." A peaceful smile formed on her lips. Wanda hadn't seen her mother's smile in years.

"Yes, delicious," her father agreed, the wrinkles in his forehead slowly smoothing away.

Wanda was deliriously happy to see that, even though she'd had to guess about the recipe, the brew she had prepared was beginning to work. She turned to Zane— and jumped up from her chair, startled.

"Very good tea, Wanda. Thank you." The eight-year-old boy-beast was gone, and in his place stood a young man of eighteen, the true Zane. Wanda didn't think it was possible, but he was even more handsome than William.

"Who's your friend, Wanda?" her mother asked. "Aren't you going to introduce us?"

"His name is Zane," Wanda replied. Her parents didn't recognize him, and she realized it would take time to explain everything to them. To avoid more questions—at least for now—she guided him out of the kitchen.

"Nice to meet you, Zane." Wanda's father waved after them. "Come back soon!"

"Zane, you're yourself again!" Wanda whispered in the living room. "And you're . . . you're . . . older." She couldn't get accustomed to the real Zane, and she tried not to stare. "How does it feel to be free of your mother's curse?"

"My mother's curse . . ." Zane said slowly, as if tasting the words. "Yes, I am free." He studied Wanda closely, with an icy stare that seemed to cut her.

Wanda took a step back. The eight-year-old Zane was a bother for sure, but this one was truly frightening. "Your brother, William, is waiting for you." She told him what had happened and instructed him to head to the cave. She encouraged him to leave at once.

"Thank you, Wanda," he said again, but with a coldness that sent a chill down her spine. He still had a dark, wild look in his eyes, and Wanda suspected it had always been there, even before his mother's spell. "I will not forget this."

She reached into her pocket and gripped the Enlightener. She knew it would protect her from him, but still, when he headed out the door, she was relieved to see him go.

THIRTY-NINE

Where's Wren?

Wanda stepped back to admire the fresh yellow paint she had just brushed on the front door.

"So cheerful." Her mother wrapped her in a warm hug.

"And the garden looks lovely." Her father, sitting on the garden bench, smiled at the magenta, purple, and golden pansies that he and Wanda had planted.

The garden did look wonderful, and Wanda was quite satisfied with all the colorful flowers they had selected, especially the pink and red blossoms the butterflies seemed to like, too. For a moment, she recalled the witches' garden, but she quickly banished it from her mind. She preferred not to think about it, not now, not ever.

This week had been the best of her life. Her parents were the family she had always dreamed of having. They were kind and thoughtful, and it was clear that they loved her very much.

"Tell us again." Her mother took a seat on the garden bench, too. "Who is Zane?"

Wanda's parents were still recovering from the spell. They couldn't fathom where the time had gone. They had no idea what had transpired over the last few years. And they were slowly remembering what their life had been like before Raymunda. Wanda felt confident that, in time, their minds would clear and their memories would return completely.

"Zane is the witch's son," Wanda explained again. Then she told them once more about her adventure in the Scary Wood and the ghastly creatures that had attacked her.

"What a frightful time!" Her mother's face flooded with worry and horror. "You were in such danger"— she took a deep breath—"and we weren't there to help you."

"Wanda, we are so grateful to you," her father said.

"You were incredibly brave. You risked everything to return our lives to us."

"Yes." Her mother's eyes filled with tears. "Now we can be a happy family again."

Wanda's father started drawing a circle in the soil with the top of his boot, but he didn't close the loop. "I'm happy, yes, but I can't help but feel that something is missing. . . . I can't quite put my finger on what it is, though. . . ."

Just then a bird flew down to perch on the edge of the birdbath. Wanda was disappointed, as always these days, that it wasn't Voltaire.

"Mother," said Wanda, "have you seen any bluebirds around lately?"

"Bluebirds?" Her mother shook her head. "No, just robins and sparrows."

"Birds . . ." Wanda's father murmured. "I think it has something to do with a bird." He stared up into the tree as if the missing thing might be hidden up there. Then he jumped to his feet. "That's it! How could we have forgotten? Wren!"

Wanda's mother stood up and cast a frantic glance left and right. Then behind her. "Wren! Yes! Where is Wren?"

For a moment, Wanda was confused. Why were her parents searching for a wren? *Oh, wait,* Wanda realized. *Not a bird. A person.* The name seemed familiar to her, but she couldn't recall exactly where she had heard it. "Who?" Wanda asked.

"Wren!" her mother replied. "Your sister!"

FORTY

It Started with a Thud

*I*t has been one week and five hours since I returned home from the Scary Wood. It's wonderful here without Zane. But today I learned that I have a sister. She's one year older than me, and her name is Wren. She's been gone so long I don't remember anything about her. When I see her, it will be like meeting her for the first time.

It could be excellent to have a big sister. But since I'm a very honest person, I have to admit it would be much better if I didn't have to rescue her from a witch. Is that unkind? I don't want to be mean again. Still, I wish that there was someone else who would go save her instead. My parents are too frightened to do it. They *say there has to be another way, but so far they haven't come up with it yet. And anyway, it would be too dangerous for them. They're still in a daze from Raymunda's spell.*

When they look at me, they see me now. They see who I am, and they are proud of me. But they also see what's missing. Each time they look at me, I am a reminder that they have another daughter who is gone. It shows in their eyes.

So now I must return to the Scary Wood. I just packed my dragon sweater and hat and Voltaire's, too, in case I should see him. I'm ready to go, but I'm having a hard time with the actual leaving. Raymunda wants me dead, and I'm headed her way, and I think that would be enough for anyone to decide to stay home. But my parents need Wren, and Wren needs me to find her.

Wanda continued to write in her diary—but stopped when she heard a loud *THUD.* She looked up to see a little blue lump crumpled on her windowsill.

Voltaire!

She leaped up from her bed, opened the window, and scooped up the bird.

"Voltaire, are you all right?" She held him up to see if he was breathing. Then she set him down on her dresser, and he opened his eyes. He bent his neck from side to side, fanned his feathers, and stood up.

"My neck is a bit stiff, but that seems to be the worst of it. Wanda, dear, if I'm going to be visiting, you might think about keeping the window open."

"I'm so happy to see you! I have something to tell you—the girl dressed in yellow? The one in my visions? She's my sister, Wren! And we think that Raymunda is holding her prisoner! I'm about to sneak off to go look for her."

"Wren? What a coincidence! That's why I am here! So good of you to remind me." He started to pace back and forth across the dresser. "I have discovered that there is a girl with the witch—and she is your sister. Oh. You know this already. Not very helpful, I suppose."

"But it *is* helpful! The witch has Wren—now we're sure of it," Wanda said.

"Hold on! There's something more you should know." Voltaire stopped his pacing and looked into Wanda's eyes. "And you should know it before you leave."

"What is it?" Wanda asked.

"It's . . . Let me see . . . Wait. . . . I knew it when I left, but apparently I have arrived without it. No worries, dear Wanda. We shall go off together, posthaste, to find Wren . . . and along the journey, I'm almost certain I'll remember it."

Wanda smiled. She grabbed her rucksack from the bed and hefted it over her shoulder. "If we do not find anything pleasant, at least we shall find something new."

"How true! I couldn't have said it better myself!" Voltaire chirped, then flew out the window. "Follow me!"

Wanda leaped down the stairs two at a time to join her friend.

Voltaire's Acknowledgments

I would like to acknowledge me, the world-famous Voltaire, for all of my wonderful and witty quotes that you found in this book. It was a pleasure to share them with you and my dear Wanda. I created them back in the 1700s, but there isn't a bit of dust on them. Here they are again. Take another look:

"Doubt is not a pleasant condition.
But certainty is an absurd one."

"The longer we dwell on our misfortunes,
the greater is their power to harm us."

"If we do not find anything pleasant,
at least we shall find something new."

"The biggest reward for a thing
well done is to have done it."

"One should always aim at being
interesting rather than exact."

"The most important decision you
make is to be in a good mood."

And I would like to acknowledge you, dear reader, for reading all the way to this very page. I am going to thank you personally . . . just as soon as I can remember your name. . . .

Author's Acknowledgments

One morning, I was staring out the window of my office when I saw a bird fluttering nearby. My window was shut, and the bird was heading right for it . . . and that's where Wanda's story began. I sat down at my computer and quickly wrote the first page of this book. Then I read it to my friend and colleague Jane Stine. What ensued was a very high-level editorial discussion.

I said, "Do you think this could be something?"

Jane said, "It could definitely be something."

As you can see, Jane and I speak the same language. I can't thank her enough for her enthusiasm and encouragement from that first page to the last draft.

Pat Fortunato, Diana Guiseppone, and Ellen Steiber read the second draft, offered sage advice, and didn't even complain when I asked if they could read any faster. True friendship.

My husband, Lou Venezia, was there for all the drafts. I trust his judgment because he has the heart of a ten-year-old and the mind of a scholar, although he might say it's the other way around. Lou read every single draft, and he was required to listen when I read them aloud, and yet he remained enthusiastic, supportive, and in a pretty good mood. I would have to say that's true love.

Abraham Lurie, Leila Lurie, and Ryan Lorello, my father, sister, and nephew, are always there for me no matter what, and I think they think I'm much better at this than I really am, which can carry a person a long way, believe me.

In addition to writing, I also edit children's books. One of the authors I work with is the brilliant R. L. Stine, who has instilled a love of reading in kids all around the world with his Goosebumps book series. I've edited nearly 150 Goosebumps books so far, and along the way I've learned a thing or two from Bob about storytelling. I hope it shows. I'm very grateful.

Thank you so much to Wanda Seasongood's amazing illustrator, Jenn Harney. Working with Jenn has been total magic. Her artwork is incredible, and I can't imagine Wanda any other way. And thanks to designer Tyler Nevins for making this book look spectacular. And much appreciation to everyone at Disney Hyperion!

Which brings me to Stephanie Lurie. We're not related, but I wish we were. Stephanie is an extraordinary editor. She pinpoints with laser-like precision where a manuscript needs a second look. Her suggestions are insightful and always elevate the story. She's tireless in her review and comments, extremely patient, and incredibly polite about it all! Stephanie, thank you, thank you, thank you.

And finally . . . deepest thanks to all my elementary school teachers and librarians. They made me want to read and write. I can't imagine anything better than that.

Turn the page for a preview of

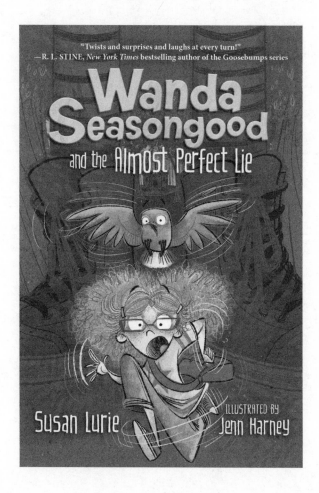

"Twists and surprises and laughs at every turn!"
—R. L. STINE, *New York Times* bestselling author of the Goosebumps series

Wanda Seasongood
and the Almost Perfect Lie

Susan Lurie

ILLUSTRATED BY
Jenn Harney

AVAILABLE NOW

ONE

A Box of Air

It was two weeks after Wanda Seasongood's eleventh birthday, and she was about to set off on a frightening mission. She stood on her porch for a moment, enjoying the warmth of the morning sun. The air felt enchanted and dreamy. *Nothing bad can happen on a day like today,* she thought. Then something fell from the sky and hit her on the head.

Wanda stumbled backward but caught herself. She quickly gazed up to see a fly zigzag above her, then zip away. Just a fly.

How peculiar.

She waited for her head to stop throbbing, then picked up the object. It was a fist-sized rock with very sharp edges. Someone had written a message on it in bold letters: **See Attached**.

See Attached? Tied to the rock was a box. *How could anyone possibly miss this?* Wanda thought as she studied it. It was slender and wrapped with plain brown paper and the thinnest twine. She lifted it close to her ear and shook it, trying to guess what was hidden inside. The package was as light as a tissue and just as silent. *A box of air,* she imagined.

What a mystery this is.

How did it suddenly fall out of the sky?

Who sent it?

Wanda wondered if it might be a birthday present. Her parents had completely forgotten her birthday, which, at the time, had been fairly upsetting. But Wanda wasn't the sort to brood about such things. Still, she'd welcome a gift from them, no matter how late or strange its arrival.

Her eyes squinted behind her brown eyeglasses as she tried to read the small writing on the package. Her name appeared on one side, but the wrapping held no other clues.

She turned the box around and around, then gazed into the trees, searching for her best friend. He was a bluebird, and as odd as it might sound, she liked talking things over with him.

Now, before you judge Wanda as weird or eccentric, you should know that this was no ordinary bluebird. His name was Voltaire, and he could speak.

Long ago, in the 1700s, there lived a man named Voltaire, a well-known French writer. But the bluebird insisted that *he* was the real Voltaire, and since he could talk and quote the famous writer, it seemed somewhat petty to object to his claim. Besides, even though the bird was often befuddled, he was very wise . . . at least Wanda thought so.

I wonder where he is? Wanda sighed. He had told Wanda he'd be back in a minute, but that was half an hour ago. *I hope he hasn't forgotten about our mission.* Which she knew was entirely possible, since he was terribly absent-minded. But a fluttering through the trees quickly put her mind at ease.

"Ah! There you are!" she said as the bird landed on a nearby shrub.

"Sorry for the delay!" he apologized. "I returned just as soon as I remembered that I had forgotten where I was going."

"Well, you came back just in time!" Wanda said. "This

fell from the sky and hit me in the head." She held up the rock and the box.

"How exciting, Wanda! You've received a special delivery. Let's open it up and see what it is!"

Wanda studied the box and the pointy edges of the rock, now convinced that it wasn't from her parents. "I don't know . . ." Her voice trailed off. "What if it's dangerous?"

"Then *I* will open it, dear Wanda!" The bird flew from the bush and settled on her arm. He started to peck at the twine's knot to loosen it. "There's no time to waste. We will do this quickly so we can be on our way. We must . . ." The bird raised his head. "Please remind me: What is it that we must do?"

"We're going to save my sister, Wren, who has been kidnapped by Raymunda, an evil witch."

"Exactly! An unforgettable mission of the highest priority!" The bluebird inflated his chest to match the enormity of the task. "And frightening."

Wanda nodded. Frightening, indeed.

It was still hard for her to believe that witches were real. And that they lived in the woods so close to her home. And that she had actually fought one of them just weeks ago.

But it was true.

Wanda and Voltaire had ventured into the Scary Wood, searching for clues to uncover a family secret. Her parents had been acting strangely, especially when it came to Zane, her horrible, beastly eight-year-old brother, whom they seemed to prefer over her. She was determined to find out why.

In the forest, Wanda had made an amazing discovery—Zane wasn't her brother! He was Raymunda's son, and even more powerful than his mother, which Raymunda could not abide. So she'd turned him into a beast-boy, bewitched the Seasongoods to accept him as their own, and stolen Wanda's older sister in a trade.

To set things straight, Wanda had battled Raymunda and escaped with a potion that would break the spells and cure Zane and her parents. When the curse was lifted, Wanda discovered that Zane wasn't a child of eight, but a young man of eighteen, and she was very relieved to see him return to his home in the woods.

"Wanda, I now recall that I was supposed to tell you something about this mission," Voltaire said, shaking Wanda from her thoughts. "I do wish I could remember what it was."

Wanda wished he could remember what it was, too. Earlier that morning, he had mentioned it. He said it was something important that she should know *before* they left to rescue Wren. But at the moment his memory held no more than that.

"I'm sure it will come back to you." Wanda hid her disappointment with a gentle smile.

"Now, as for this package . . ." Voltaire began to peck at it again.

"Voltaire, wait." Wanda lifted her arm so she could speak eye to eye with the bird. "I don't think we should open it. Raymunda might have sent it, which means whatever's inside could possibly kill us."

"We cannot allow fear to rule our lives!" Voltaire stood firm. And before she could stop him, he pulled the string free with his beak. Then he ripped the paper from the package.

"Can this really be?" Wanda blinked hard as she held up the box. "Have you ever seen anything like this?" It was made of the thinnest, most delicate threads of silver and gold, braided and shimmering, and tightly woven to form a stiff, sturdy box. She searched for a lid or a latch, but there was none. "There's no way to open it."

"Let me try!" The bluebird pecked the top of the box— and his beak sank right through the strong mesh. When he lifted his head, the surface was solid again, with no sign that he had punctured it.

"It's magical! How marvelous!" he chirped. "Can you

See Attached!

believe it? My beak has suddenly acquired new powers!"
His eyes crossed as he peered down at it with newfound
respect.

"I don't think this has anything to do with your beak."
Wanda pushed down on the top of the box, and as she

expected, it moved under her touch. It was firm enough to hold its shape yet yielded to pressure—and this gave Wanda an excellent idea.

She pressed the top of the box again, harder this time—and her fingers sank inside. She wrapped them around an object and lifted it out.

It was a gleaming silver pen with the head of a horned goat at the top. It was beautiful and seemed practically weightless. Wanda thought that if she released her grip, the pen would float out of her hand. It was very unusual and a perfect gift for Wanda, who loved to read and to write in her journal.

She sat down and slipped her purple rucksack from her shoulders. "I have to try it." She took out her diary and started to print her name.

The pen didn't work.

She tried again.

Not a single letter appeared.

And this worried her. If the pen didn't write, what *did* it do? Surely, no one who meant well would send her an unusable pen. She stared into the silvery eyes of the goat—and they seemed to stare back at her. *Where did you come from?* she wondered. *Are you an innocent gift or not?*

Wanda had known that searching for Wren would

bring trouble. But she didn't expect it this soon, or that it would land on her doorstep.

And this gave her a reason to rethink their mission. "Voltaire, I've just decided to put off the search for Wren. We should come up with another way to save her."

She attempted to use the pen again, drawing inkless whorls and swirls. "My decision is final." She gazed up at Voltaire, who was perched on the windowsill.

"Wanda, I don't want to argue with you—but the pen seems to disagree." The bird nodded toward her diary.

There, on the paper where Wanda had drawn her invisible loops, letters had taken shape. She held her breath as they continued to form. The last letter was completed with a curl and a swish. Wanda gasped as she read the message:

Wren in Danger.
Leave at Once.

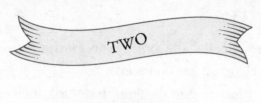

TWO

The Work of a Witch

L et's go!" At the sight of the message, Wanda's
doubts dissolved in an instant. She sprang to her
feet, tossed the pen and diary into her rucksack,
and leaped off the front steps. She was halfway down
the path to the street when she heard her mother calling.

"Wanda! Where are you going?"

Her parents stood in the doorway in their dull red
bathrobes. Her mother's hair, usually bouncy, was
pressed flat to her head. Her father's eyes were still
glazed with sleep.

"Oh, no. We have to turn back," Wanda told the bird.
"I'll make it quick."

"Where are you going so early in the morning?" Her mother shuffled down the walk to meet her.

"Were you trying to sneak out?" her father asked, puzzled.

Wanda took a deep breath. "I'm going to find Wren."

"No! No! No!" Wanda's father dove down the steps and took Wanda by the shoulders. "We've already discussed this. Fighting a witch is just too dangerous. And you shouldn't go into the woods alone."

Truth be told, Wanda wished that someone else would go save her sister. And who could blame her? After all, would *you* want to fight a witch who wanted you dead? Not likely.

And besides, Wanda barely knew her sister. Wren had been stolen so long ago, Wanda couldn't recall a thing about her. But Wanda's parents were too frightened to battle Raymunda—so that left it up to Wanda. She remembered how proud and surprised her parents had been when she returned home from the Scary Wood the first time. It was just the encouragement she needed to face the witch now.

Wanda's mother tugged the ends of her belt, tightening her robe, then clasped her daughter's hand. "Please don't go. You and Wren are very different," she said.

"We worry about you making it out of those woods again . . ."

My mother loves me so much. Wanda's heart swelled with well-being.

" . . . because you were never the smart one," Mrs. Seasongood went on. "You might not be as lucky this time."

Wanda's shoulders sagged and her knees buckled. Her heart was instantly crushed, her determination pummeled, and she was, quite frankly, too stunned to reply. She took a deep breath and instructed herself to focus on what was important—finding Wren.

"You're probably right," Wanda said when the shock had dulled and she could finally speak. "It's too dangerous." Then she headed to the garden at the back of her house.

The moment Wanda's parents lost sight of her, she vaulted over the backyard fence with Voltaire flying closely behind her. She ran through the leafy streets and up a deserted hill. She ran through a small town. She ran as fast as she could to flee from her mother's insult. She ran until she reached a meadow at the edge of the Scary Wood. Only then did she stop to catch her breath.

"My parents think I'm stupid, Voltaire. I never knew

they thought so little of me." Her mother's words had cut very deep.

"Don't be upset." The bluebird landed on her shoulder. "Your parents want to keep you safe. They simply lack tact."

"Wait. What are you saying?" Wanda's head whipped around sharply. Her frizzy reddish-brown hair whacked the bird and sent him hurling into the air.

"Tact, Wanda," Voltaire said, fluttering safely to the ground. "It's 'the knack of making a point without making an enemy'—to quote my good friend Sir Isaac Newton."

"No. No. Are *you* saying that I'm not smart?"

"I don't think I'm saying that at all...." Voltaire brought the top of his wing to his chin. "Hmm...Is Wanda smart?" Head down, he paced the sidewalk,

contemplating the question. "Aha!" He stopped and lifted his head. "I would have to be smart to know the answer to that. Do you think *I'm* smart?"

"Yes, of course I do," she answered.

"Thank you, Wanda. Smart of you to say so. There! That settles that! Now, let's carry on." He rose from the ground and flew into the woods.

Wanda stepped from a field of bright, cheerful goldenrod into the forest's black shifting shadows, and a feeling of dread passed through her. Everything about these woods was disturbing—the musty smell that choked her breath, the darkness that snuffed out the morning light, the eerie, evil stillness. . . .

She thought about some of the creatures she had met the last time she was here. The Groods—horrible beasts who had tried to tear her apart limb from limb. The swamp creature, a gnome who had turned her to smoke. The nixie, a water spirit who had attempted to drown her. She shuddered.

"Nothing good happens in these woods," she murmured.